Bedtime Erotica

for

MEN

Lexy Harper

Bedtime Erotica

for

MEN

Ebonique Publishing

Please practise safe sex.

All characters in this publication are fictitious and any resemblance to real persons, living or dead, is purely coincidental.

The author and publisher specifically disclaim any responsibility for any liability, loss or risk, which is incurred as a consequence, directly or indirectly, of the use and application of any of the contents of this book.

The text of this publication or any part thereof may not be reproduced or transmitted in any form or by any means, electronic or mechanical, including photocopying, recording, storage in an information retrieval system, or otherwise, without the written permission of the publisher or author, except for brief quotes used in reviews.

First published in Great Britain 2008

Published by Ebonique Publishing, London.
ISBN-13: 978-0-9556986-3-7

CONTENTS

To the men who inspired these *fucking* stories.

PERFECT SCORE

*H*er broad bottom threatened to burst the seams of her Burberry skirt as she bent over her desk to check the faulty connection at the back of her computer. He should be a gentleman and do it for her. He really should. But as soon as she'd bent over, Mason's cock had become as hard as a rock, he couldn't move away from his desk if a fire suddenly broke out in the building.

Her virginal pussy must be so tight!

Hailey Ambrose was one of the ugliest young women he had ever seen. Okay, she wasn't ugly but she was a big girl and the fact that she didn't go to a gym or do any form of exercise didn't help. Neither did her weakness for Bahlsen Choco Leibniz Dark Chocolate biscuits. She was close to two hundred pounds and at 5'10" that made her well over the recommended BMI. Women had to look after themselves—she wasn't even twenty-five years old and she had already let herself go—he would hate to see her when she hit forty. He shuddered at the thought.

But she stood between Mason and his 100% record.

Last year the guys in the office had crowned him Office Player after he had bedded eight of their fifteen female colleagues within six months of being employed by the company. He had continued his successful campaign at the start of the current year and taken another five scalps by April.

Then the real challenge had begun.

The two remaining females tested his sexual prowess in different ways: one, his supervisor, cool beauty Mrs Eleanor Trotz, was like Fort Knox; the other, Hailey was so fat he would be ashamed to admit fucking her.

Eleanor's husband Brendan was the Managing Director of the company, fucking her had inherent risks. They had married when she had fallen pregnant at the age of seventeen, yet it was impossible to imagine the mother-of-three having sex. Most people were convinced that she'd had sex just three times in her life—once for each pregnancy. Others believed that she'd in fact had sex only *once* but had stored the sperm in her below-zero womb until she had deemed it time for the next conception to occur. She was fondly referred to as the Ice Maiden.

Two days ago Mason had finally gotten her into his bed or rather on top of her desk. He had gone into her office on the pretext of getting her approval of the rough draft for the beer commercial he was working on. For the umpteenth time he had complimented her on her sexy body and innate dress style before telling her that he dreamt of her constantly. She had coolly assessed him for a minute or two without saying a word and he had wondered if he had finally gone too far. He'd been flirting with her for months but had been careful to avoid saying anything that could be considered sexual harassment. He had quickly apologized, gathered his materials and gotten up to leave. She had let him walk as far as the door before she'd said, "Come and see me when the others have left this evening."

He had loitered in the office, his head down, concentrating furiously on his computer screen as his colleagues had left one after the other, surprised at his sudden enthusiasm. Hailey had been the last to leave. Her 'Good night...have fun, Mason,' had dripped with sarcasm.

He had immediately gone into Eleanor's office, his hard cock begging to be freed from the confinement of his boxers. Eleanor had stood up and appraised him from head to toe, noting the big bulge in his trousers that he'd made no attempt to conceal.

"Right, you have fifteen minutes," she'd said as if he was going to give her a presentation of his latest idea, not fuck her.

Mason, never one to stand on ceremony, had rounded the desk and wrapped his arms around her. Her tall, lithe body had felt great pressed against him. He had kissed her deeply while unbuttoning her silk blouse and expertly freeing her full, firm breasts. He had immediately pulled one of her erect nipples into his mouth and sucked on it, hard. Most women would have at that point pressed his head against their breast—Eleanor simply stood with her hands hanging limply at her sides. Conscious of the passing time he'd slid his hand under her skirt and encountered her bare pussy. She'd been wet and fearful that it would be time-out before he got his cock inside her, he had pushed her back onto the desk and freed his cock. She'd looked at it as though it was nothing special and it had pissed him off.

So the bitch wants to play, he'd thought angrily and had swung her legs onto his broad shoulders and proceeded to fuck her as hard as he could.

She hadn't completely unthawed during the onslaught but her pussy had gradually unfrozen until it had almost reached room temperature by the time he'd ground himself deep inside her and cum. He had glanced at the clock on the wall as he'd pulled his cock free. Almost timed to perfection—sixteen minutes from taking her in his arms to cumming with a big bang!

Her conquest had exalted him to Player of the Century. His awed but envious workmates had demanded every last detail. He had taken great pleasure in describing her firm, lush body—including the map-of-Barbados birthmark on her upper thigh and the way she hadn't moved her waist or made a sound even when he had plunged his big cock into her tight, lukewarm pussy with a single, hard thrust. They had been incredulous when he'd told them that after she'd straightened her clothes, she had taken £250 out of her purse, put it on her desk and left without saying a single word.

The guys didn't expect him to fuck fat Hailey. As far as they were concerned he was The Man: he came to work for the company; he saw the beautiful women and he conquered them all. Well, all the 'fuckable' ones anyway.

But unconquered Hailey bugged Mason. Even if he had to put a paper bag over her head he was going to fuck her. He just had to!

The women at the last company he had worked, a very prestigious West End firm, hadn't been nearly as accommodating. He had only scored with a dismal 30% of them. Most men would have been satisfied with his current score of above 90% but for Mason it was too close to perfection. He had to go for the perfect score—100% or die trying.

Hailey was bending even more dangerously forward. He should really help her. He checked the status of his crotch. Half-mast—shouldn't be too noticeable. He got up and walked over to her desk, deliberately brushing against her as he quickly found the loose connection and shoved it firmly into its USB socket.

"Thanks Mason." Her big breasts were almost touching his chest as she turned to thank him, but she didn't move away. She was at least a G or H cup, her big nipples visible through her flimsy bra. Sadly he suspected, unlike a compass point, her nipples pointed south rather than north.

"You owe me one," he whispered and headed for the gents.

Hurrying into the nearest cubicle, he leaned back against the door, whipped out his erect cock and started to wank.

There was something about her that got to him. Something that eroded his common sense. Something that got his cock rock-hard against his will. Something...okay, okay, it was her virginity...the thought of potentially being the one to pop her cherry drove him insane. He cursed himself for not following through after the Christmas party. She had stood with the rest of her female colleagues, sipping wine all night. One by one the guys had dragged the other women to the dance floor but no one had asked Hailey. Feeling charitable and a little drunk after several bottles of beer he had gone over and pulled her on to the floor for an up-beat number. She had shaken her big breasts and fat ass with a lot more enthusiasm than he had expected and hadn't looked as ugly in the softer light of the wine bar. He had been contemplating making her his ninth scalp when Jessica, his fifth, came over and whispered that her ass was vacant for the night. Her husband who worked for Charlton Athletic FC, was out of town on business and her son was spending the night with her parents.

No man alive could turn down the chance to fuck buck-toothed, freaky Jessica's ass, again.

And that night she'd been in an extra freaky mood. As soon as they had entered his flat she had unzipped his fly, pulled out his already hard cock and given him head while she had dipped her fingers in her pussy for some lubrication and started to prepare her ass for penetration. Within minutes he had her bent over the back of his leather armchair as he held her cheeks apart and forced his cock inside her. She'd moaned and groaned as he'd sunk it deeper and deeper but she'd admitted to him the first time that she liked pain so he gave her as much as he could. She had also told him that her husband fucked her ass regularly but his limp dick was almost half the size of his. They had then moved to his king-sized bed where he had knelt behind her and continued the ass-fucking. They had both slept soundly until the middle of the next day but as soon as he had gotten up and had his morning pee, he slid back under the duvet and attacked her ass again. Jessica had taken a cab from his place late that evening, her ass so well-buttered she'd said that she would have to wait at least a week before she dared allow her husband to push his much smaller dick inside it again without arousing his suspicions.

When Mason had returned to work the following Monday and seen Hailey in the brightly-lit office he'd been relieved that he hadn't fucked her. Jessica's ass had saved his. He'd decided there and then that Hailey would be the last of his scalps. No sense in fucking her if any of the six remaining women didn't free up her pussy. He would fuck her only if needs be.

Now needs be—he was going to fuck her!

He had to walk back past Hailey's desk to get to his. She smiled knowingly as he approached, her dark eyes quickly sweeping down to his crotch and back up to meet his.

No way she could have known he'd just had a wank!

Yet, somehow he had a strong feeling she did.

But how the hell could she?

Maybe she was psychic, she had a weird way of knowing a lot more than she reasonably should. Every time he had sniffed around a female colleague she seemed to know he was after pussy. Twice when he had come back to his desk after achieving another scalping with a quick tumble in the stationery cupboard, she'd looked at him as though she'd known exactly what and whom he'd been doing. Both times he and the female colleague in question had carefully planned their tryst and everyone but Hailey had been blissfully unaware that some fucking had occurred under their noses. Her parting shot the day he had fucked Eleanor was clear proof that nothing seemed to escape her rapier gaze.

She was still smiling as he went past her desk.

What if she decided to blackmail him with the knowledge, threaten to tell Eleanor's husband that he had fucked the man's wife? He stopped in mid-stride, momentarily paralyzed by the thought, then he shook his head and smiled. Nah! Hailey was fat but she was cool, she knew how to keep her mouth shut. Plus she fancied Mason like crazy, although she didn't dare hope that the best-looking guy in the office would give her a second glance. None of the other guys did and there were a few almost as ugly as Hailey herself. At least they dressed in the style suited to an advertising agency, unlike her. Not only was she fat but she had a very quirky dress style. She didn't wear sober designer suits like the rest of the staff—both male and female—she wore loud, vibrant colours. Which would have been fine if she was slim but she was a big girl and the last thing she needed was to call attention to herself. Her nails were always perfectly manicured and she spent a fortune on shoes. Her feet were well shaped and surprisingly slim for a woman of her size. He always expected to hear the sound of one of her stiletto heels snapping under her weight as she marched across the office floor with her purposeful, large-and-in-charge, hip-swaying stride. Her thick, expertly-trimmed, straightened hair was the sexiest thing on her, it bounced with every movement she made and looked shiny and healthy. Against his will, Mason sometimes imagined running his hand through the lustrous strands as she gave him head. She wasn't afraid to dress sexily and show tons of cleavage. The red halter dress she had worn to the Christmas party had been scandalous! That evening she had swapped her usual French manicure for a shade of red that perfectly matched her dress and her sexy high-heeled shoes. She'd looked liked an overweight hooker. She *did* make an effort with her appearance, it was a pity that she didn't take it one step further and go to the gym.

Her colleagues had a strange relationship with her, the women liked her—probably because she wasn't a threat; the guys treated her with surprising respect which was odd in an office where the staff were mostly under the age of thirty. The guys constantly teased each other and all the other women in the office, but none of them ever teased Hailey. They treated her as if they were afraid she would beg them for a sympathy fuck. She didn't socialize with any colleagues outside of the office, yet she seemed to know a lot about what went on in the company.

***

"Hi Mason!"

The chirpy female voice startled him as he opened the door of his Mazda MX-8 Nemesis and slid onto the driver's seat.

"What the fu—?" he broke off as the overweight object of his earlier wank in the gents straightened from her crouched position in the back seat. "Hailey, what are you doing in my fucking car? Scaring the hell out of me?"

"You said I owed you one. I was hoping that you would come around to my house tonight so I could give it to you."

"You can't handle my big cock!" he told her scornfully.

"I could…if you made me very wet first." She fluttered the thick lashes of her myopic eyes at him.

She was as blind as a bat without her glasses.

Did she take them off when she went to bed?

The thought of her naked, except for her thick glasses,

rekindled a boyhood fantasy he had long forgotten. At the age of fifteen he had masturbated almost nightly thinking of his stern, bespectacled English teacher, Mrs Allen, naked, peeping over her glasses at him as she wrapped her prim mouth around his cock and gave him head.

"What's your address?" he asked, feeling his cock harden.

She pulled a card from between her breast and handed it to him. "I've been keeping it warm for you."

The card was slightly damp and he almost dropped it in disgust.

She could probably drown a fly between those melons.

"See you at eight. Don't be late." She swung her huge thighs out of the car in a graceful motion and got out. The car immediately lifted and he heard the suspension breathe a sigh of relief.

He smelled the card cautiously thinking he would not bother to turn up if she stank. The most alluring scent filled his nostrils. He pressed it against his nose and took a deeper breath. Light, expensive, floral perfume mixed with another scent—the fragrance of woman, in heat—an aroma he knew well.

He glanced at his watch. Only five thirty-five. Shit! He would need another wank when he got home; the thought of her tight, never-plundered pussy was sending him into overdrive.

***

She answered the door as soon as he pressed the buzzer at quarter to eight, dressed in a belted robe. The waistband was drawn tightly around her trim waist making her hips and breasts look much larger in comparison—doing her no favours, Mason silently observed.

She didn't appear to be wearing a negligee or any such garment under the robe. Probably didn't come in her size. Would it still be called a negligee in a size 16/18? Mason had no idea, he had only ever bought lingerie in a size 10.

Hailey looked surprisingly cool and composed for a young woman about to have her cherry plucked. Mason smiled. She won't be as cool when she saw the size of his cherry-plucker.

"Hi Hailey," he said as he stepped into the hallway. She smiled and backed up to let him enter. He hadn't bothered to bring her a bunch of roses, a bottle of wine or a box of chocolates as he usually would when going to a woman's home for the first time. Personally he felt Hailey should be the one wining and dining him, not the other way around.

"Hi Mason, I'm so glad you came—I was afraid you'd change your mind."

"I'm a man of my word. If I say I'll do something, I do it."

"I didn't doubt your integrity," she quickly assured him. "I didn't give you advance notice and I thought you might have had a prior engagement that you may have forgotten when we spoke this evening."

"I cancelled it," he lied. No point in letting her know that the only plan he'd had for the evening was going to a bar somewhere in the West End and trying to pick up a woman.

"What would you like to drink? I have a large selection," she said as she turned and walked into her enormous living room.

He looked around the room in surprise. Her annual salary, like his, must hit the high six-figure mark with the generous bonuses the company had been giving out due to the team's increased efficiency but there was no way that his salary would stretch to maintain the lifestyle she seemed to have. He was still reeling from the surprise of driving up to the large, semi-detached house with the same address as the business card she had given him.

"What did you do, Hailey? Rob a bank or win the fucking lottery?" He made no attempt to hide the envy in his voice.

"I have a small but very lucrative business," she informed him.

He waited for her to elaborate, she didn't. But he didn't question her further. He would turn on the charm while he was fucking her or just afterwards, when the memory of it was still fresh in her mind and she would tell him everything. He wouldn't leave her house before she made him a partner in whatever business deal she had going unless it was something illegal. Even then, it would depend on *how* illegal.

She pulled a section of wooden panelling back to reveal a drink selection that made his eyes almost pop out of his head. Turning to look at him enquiringly she asked, "What's your tipple?"

"I'll have a double JD please."

It won't harm to be a little tipsy when I fuck you.

She must have read his thoughts because the shot she poured him was more like a treble.

"You don't mind if I only have cranberry juice?" she queried. "I had a brandy earlier to steady my nerves."

That's why the bitch is so cool.

"No problem. I would hate for you to get drunk and fall asleep on me." He meant it literally as well as figuratively. She must weigh a ton.

"I wouldn't do that!" she protested. "I have been dying for you to come over to my place. I'm ecstatic now you're here."

"You should be. It isn't often I give up a Friday night for *any* woman," he lied again. She couldn't know that his Friday nights were spent in the pursuit of fresh pussy.

"I'm very honoured."

The robe slipped slightly and revealed the smooth, upper

slopes of her breasts. She was wearing one of those flimsy bras again—her nipples poked through the towelling robe.

"Mason, I know that you are used to making love to beautiful, sexy women—I'm very grateful that you are doing me this great honour. In recognition of this I don't mind if you prefer not to see my face when you are on top of me."

She was going to bag her own face? Unbelievable!

"I think a blindfold would be best," she continued.

Not as good as a paper bag but good enough.

"Hailey, I don't really need the blindfold, but I'll wear it…if you insist."

"Mason, you are very kind but I don't want you to lose your erection at the sight of my fat face."

He opened his mouth to deny her words but closed it again. She had accepted her ugly fatness—false compliments were unnecessary.

"Do you mind if I sucked you first?" she asked innocently.

"*Sucked* me?" He almost choked on his JD.

"I mean give you a…a blowjob," she clarified and covered her face in embarrassment.

"I don't mind at all."

"I'm not sure that I'll be very good but whenever I watch videos the women always do it to the men."

She watched porn? Well, well, well!

"I'm sure you'll do a great job," he assured her. "I'll give you instructions if necessary."

"Thanks, Mason. You're being so good about this. Most times the men in the videos don't suck the women in return so I won't expect you to suck me."

"Oral sex is different for a man. He has to deal with the smell and the thought that a woman gets periods. I feel like being sick when I do it," he lied. No point in going down on her if he didn't have to.

"Most of the men in the videos also take the women from the back. Is that what you would do to me?"

"From the back…?"

Was she talking about ass-fucking?

"Yes, sometimes the men take their penises out of the women's front and push it into their back passage," Hailey clarified. "It seems to happen in every video I watch. Would we do that too? I wouldn't mind if you did—the men seem to enjoy it very much."

"Hailey, it's a part of sex." He barely managed to keep a straight face. "For a man to feel *real* pleasure he must fuck a woman's pussy as well as her ass."

"Okay," she agreed without hesitation.

Naïve fat bitch! I'm going to pluck both fucking cherries!

"Take your clothes off so that I can suck your penis," she instructed. "I won't take off my robe until you are wearing the blindfold."

"No problem." He stood up to start undressing and found that he was a little unsteady on his feet.

Hold back on the JD, my son, he warned himself.

He debated for a second whether or not to leave his boxers on, then thought, *what the hell?* and pulled it off too.

"Oh Mason, you look better than the guys in my videos. I've always wanted a man with a big penis—yours is nice and big. I like the fact that you are not circumcised too. I've read that the man gets more pleasure if he has a foreskin."

"Yes, a penis with its foreskin intact is much more sensitive than one without," he confirmed.

She had done her homework.

Although he wasn't totally surprised, she was easily the most successful staff member in the agency. She had received a first class honours in Applied Business Management from Imperial College and the company had quickly snapped her up. Almost every time Mr Trotz gathered the staff for a brain-storming session when the company scooped a major advertising campaign, Hailey would be the one to come up with the most unique, inspired ideas. Mason suspected that she spent her spare time doing research, since it was unlikely that any man would date her. At least none with good taste.

"Shall we go up to the bedroom?" she suggested.

"Why not?"

He may as well get the fucking over and done with.

She held out a chubby hand, he grasped it and was surprised how incredibly soft it was. She kept hold of his hand as they made their way up the stairs.

"I can't wait to suck you," she said, turning to face him as they entered the bedroom.

He felt as if he'd stepped into a page of Hello! or OK Magazine. The four-poster bed was the kind you'd expect to see in a harem. It was draped with fine netting and pillows of varying sizes and shapes were placed neatly against the ornate, carved wooden headboard. He started to wonder if she actually lived in the house or had rented it to impress him.

"I don't have anything or anyone else to spend my money on, so I spend it on my house," she explained as he looked around. "Let me blindfold you, I am eager to see your cock when it is erect."

"It will only get erect if you do a good job sucking it."

Nicely done, Mason! If he didn't get an erection she would think that it was her fault, not his!

"OK." She stood behind him and tied a black silk scarf around his eyes. "Comfortable?"

"Perfect!" Not too tight. Not loose enough to slip while he was fucking her.

She circled both of his wrists with her hands and kissed his palms. Then he felt something cool replace her hands and heard a distinct clicking sound. Handcuffs! Before he knew what was happening his shackled hands were attached to one of the sturdy wooden posts of the bed, his legs were trapped under her weight and she was handcuffing his right leg to the bed. He instinctively kicked out with his left but he couldn't shift her weight. Pinned by her mass his leg was no match for the surprising power in her arms. She slipped the handcuffs onto his left leg, gave a satisfied sigh and got off the bed.

"Take these handcuffs off me, Hailey!" he screamed angrily. "Take them off me now, you fucking bitch!"

"Smile for the camera, Mason darling." She took several shots of him with her instant camera, blinded and helpless, before he thought to avert his face. "Looking away won't make a difference, darling. I am sure *all* the girls in the office, including Mrs Trotz, will recognize your cock. Maybe, even some of the *guys*?"

"I'm not a faggot!" he snarled in denial. *Disrespecting my manhood! Ugly fucking bitch!*

"The word is homosexual, Mason darling. Tsk! Tsk! Not very PC, my dear." She whipped off his blindfold. "Mr Trotz won't be happy to hear you being so derogatory about men like him. *And* you fucked his wife without his permission. You are playing with fire—cause for dismissal I'd say!"

"Mr Trotz is not gay!"

"Tell that to the men he rents from my agency and his poor wife whom he hasn't fucked in six years. Luckily, I employ straight men as well—I give them a family discount when I supply men for both of them on the same night."

"You're full of shit!" Mason yelled at her scornfully.

"Don't be embarrassed because it took you *three* whole months, of crawling like a worm, to fuck Mrs Trotz when I could have arranged for you to fuck her since last year."

Mason stared at her as if she were an alien who had just walked off a blinking UFO. "And she would have paid you a *lovely* £250 for your trouble."

His mouth opened in shock.

"Did she pay you too?" Hailey laughed. "Probably out of habit; she has been paying for her cock so long she's forgotten that some men still fuck for free. I hope you used some of it to buy a willy-warmer. My boys tell me that her pussy is like the Artic Zone—it takes days for their cocks to warm up after being inside her crypt."

How could this fat cow know so much?

"I think *she* might be the reason her husband is gay. She was the first woman the poor man fucked and the temperature of her pussy must have put him off pussies for life. I suspect he only fucked another man's ass in an attempt to warm his cock, but got hooked on the heat."

Mason's mind tried to come to grips with the thought that his squash partner was gay. For the last four months they had played for half an hour every lunchtime and afterwards shared the showers. He felt sick at the thought that the other man could have been secretly eying his cock or worst eying his fucking butt!

I'm never playing squash with that faggot again!

"I know the two of you play squash every lunchtime," Hailey said, making no effort to conceal her amusement. "I hope it means you play the game and *not* that he has you *squashed* against the wall of the court warming his cock in your ass!"

"Look bitch, I don't fuck around other men!" The fire in his eyes as he glared at her was so fierce she should have gone up in flames.

Mason had never felt more like strangling someone in his entire life. He didn't have any gay friends; he didn't understand why *any* man would look at another man's hairy ass and want to fuck it. It just didn't make any sense to him. He was homophobic and proud. Once a male colleague who 'lived in the closet' made a tentative overture in Mason's direction after they'd had several drinks in a nearby bar after work one day. Mason had nearly flattened him. The poor man had apologized profusely but Mason had been so furious at the slur to his machismo he had 'outed' his colleague the very next day. The story, however, had a surprisingly happy ending—another of their colleagues had been 'living in his own closet'. The two men got together and it pissed Mason off to see them having lunch together, staring into each other's eyes; going home together, knowing that they were going to give each other head and fuck each other's butts when they got there. If he had only known he would have kept his mouth shut. He was relieved to leave the job, and the two 'batty-men' as he called them, three months later.

Hailey ignored his rage and smiled sweetly as she asked, "By the way, who do you want your photograph to be next to in my album?"

She opened a thick album and started to flick through it. "Adrian, the toad; Angelo, the snake; Bertie, the old dog; Conrad, the cunt; David B, the pussy; David H, the asshole; George, the BO king—God, that man is so stink I had to air both my pussy and my house after he had been inside them; Jake, the pussy-licker; Mitchell, the nipple-sucker; Ne—"

"WHAT?" Mason roared as the implication of her words finally sunk in.

She had been fucked before? She wasn't a fucking virgin?

"You thought you were the first? Sorry to disappoint you, Mason, honey. I've fucked all the guys in the office, even *Simple* Simon from the post room—you're the last, darling." She smiled at him, as a mother would a confused child, before she sat on the bed close to him, holding the album so that he could see the photographs of his work colleagues—all similarly bound. "Neil was the best—the *only* one who didn't come to my home just to *use* me. The only one who made love to me without the need for torture." She smiled indulgently at his horrified expression. "Oh, didn't you know people with cerebral palsy are fantastic lovers? Neil could probably teach a *macho* man like you more about a woman's body than you would ever learn on your own."

"You fucked that freak?" Mason almost threw up at the thought of the two of them together. She would completely cover Neil if she lay on top of him.

"Now, you've really pissed me off!" She slapped him hard across the face. "Don't ever call him a freak again! He's a prince—the only reason I didn't become his mistress was because I like Lynette so much."

When Mason had met Lynette at the Christmas party, he had been amazed how drop-dead gorgeous Neil's wife was. He was even more surprised to learn that they had met only the year before she had become his wife—he had imagined she would have had to have been a childhood friend or sweetheart. And it wasn't as if Lynette needed Neil's money, she came from an upper middle-class family, too.

"I'm sorry," he mumbled as Hailey stood over him, ready to slap him again.

"Okay, I forgive you, but don't speak unless you have something pleasant to say."

She went back to turning the pages, ignoring the small trickle of blood flowing from his cut lip. "*Maybe* I'll keep it in alphabetical order."

Abruptly, she put the photo album down and took his cock into her mouth. He tried to stay immune but the sight of her giving him head still wearing her glasses was too much for him. And she was no shrinking violet either—she knew how to give head.

She pulled his hard cock from her throat and stroked it tenderly. "While other people contemplate the mysteries of the universe *I* contemplate cocks. I wonder if I sat on a rigid cock too fast if it would bend or break under my weight." She kept one hand at the base and slid the other to the tip. "I wonder if I bend one between my hands…"she applied pressure and he groaned "…if I would be strong enough to snap it." She eased the pressure and he took a deep, shaky breath. "I also wonder if I bit one…" she bent towards his rapidly deflating cock and he screamed "…if my teeth would go right through it." She sat back and looked at him. "These questions sometimes keep me up at night. I am working on several hypotheses which I will have to test on someone's cock sooner or later."

"Hailey, I'm sorry." He didn't want to be her lab rat.

"There is nothing to be sorry about. I can't blame you for assuming that I'm too fat for anyone to fuck *or* for coming over to my house to do me the huge favour of taking my virginity. I made that same assumption on my sixteenth birthday when I used an 8" dildo to pop my own cherry."

She was stark raving mad!

She stroked his now flaccid cock and continued as though *popping* a cherry was as easy as picking one off a tree, "It wasn't that painful, you know. I did some research beforehand and found out that in some tribes the young women have to do it as a 'rite of passage'. Although, I am not sure that the ceremonial stick they use is as big as the *dick* I used. I had planned to buy a 6" dildo. I wasn't too bothered about the girth as long as it was the right colour—I wanted my first man to be Black. I saw him on the shelf as soon as I walked into the sex shop. He and I had so much in common it was scary. Like me he was big—some people might have described him as 'overweight' but it's a concept I don't acknowledge, to me he was simply *well-blessed*. I walked past him but he called my name, 'Hailey, buy me, sugar. I love you, baby.' I tried to ignore him, thinking that it was a line he fed all the girls but he kept calling out to me in a lilting Guyanese accent, 'Hailey, *big* is beautiful, honey. I want to be your man, precious. I want to slide between your juicy cunt lips, niceness. I want to fuck your tight, young pussy, sweetness. *Please* let me pluck your cherry, darling.' *That's* when I knew he was the one for me. I bought him and quickly hurried out of the shop. On the way home he told me that he'd been waiting for me a long time and now that he'd found me he was going to fuck me day and night. He told me that he didn't like skinny women, said they were too vain and didn't eat enough to withstand his fucking. He told me that he was going to make me very happy—and he does, *every* day. He gets terribly lonely if I let a day go by without giving him some pussy. I call him Marley because Choice FM was playing *No Woman No Cry* the *very* first time he fucked me. I had the most fantastic first time. Marley rubbed himself all over my body. My nipples were like rocks by the time he was finished. He even made me give him a little head. Not too much. He said I was too young to really deep-throat him. When he spread my legs I was dripping but he still rubbed himself against my clit until I *begged* him to fuck me. I still remember that perfect moment when he drove himself inside me."

Mad fucking woman!

"He assured me that the bleeding was normal, especially if a girl's first man is as well-hung as he is, and he is well, *hung*. He was *so* considerate that night. He knew that I was sore so he didn't fuck me again until early the next morning. It was Sunday so we spent the whole day in bed together. Every time I tried to get up, he called me back for one last fuck. My parents kept banging on my door asking me if I was okay. Eventually, I had to let my father come in to my bedroom to check that I hadn't sneaked a boy up to my room. He checked everywhere: under the bed, in my en suite bathroom, my built-in wardrobe...everywhere except my pussy where Marley was hiding. Let me tell you, Marley was furious at being interrupted! I had been at the *crucial* moment when my father had threatened to kick the door down if I didn't unlock it. As soon as I locked the door again we went straight back to fucking."

The woman was definitely mad! She belonged in a mental institution under heavy sedation. And in a straight-jacket, in case the drugs wore off before another dose could be administered.

"Marley had this fantasy about fucking me in the shower, so we stepped into the bathroom together. He fucked me twice in there: once from the front with my right foot high up against the wall and then from the back with me bending over. We were at it like rabbits for the whole night too. He almost cried when I left for school the next day. I missed him so much I pretended to be sick and the headmistress sent me home half day. As soon as I got indoors he didn't even let me take off my school uniform, he ripped my panties and started to fuck me. He fucked me hard for hours, non-stop. Not satisfied that I had learned my lesson he pushed his head just inside my asshole as further punishment and threatened to fuck my ass *fully* if I left him home the next day. I knew my ass couldn't handle his big cock, it was sore from him pushing the tip inside my rim, so I took him to school with me the following day. We fucked in the girls' cloakroom for the whole lunch break but he was so horny I had to take him with me so he could continue fucking me during the afternoon classes. I had to sit at the back of the class with my legs wide open so that he could plunge deeply inside me. Let me tell you: it's *very* difficult for me to cum quietly when he's fucking me and that day he was still a bit angry that I had left him home the previous day, so he was really punishing my pussy but the thought of a teacher confiscating him made me bite my lips and keep my moans in. Luckily we wore navy skirts to school because by the end of the day the back of mine was absolutely drenched with the numerous orgasms he had given me."

She closed her eyes and her fat face became soft and dreamy.

"It's true what they say about a girl and her first man— she will always love him. We have been together for eight years and we are still so in love with each other it is sickening. He never gets tired of fucking me and he *never* gets tired. Once I'm in the house he wants to fuck me. I never have time to do any housework so I pay a skinny maid to come in weekdays and clean the house. The first maid I hired was *well-blessed* like me but the very first day she started the job I came home and found Marley fucking her ass. I had left him in my lingerie drawer so she wouldn't come across him accidentally while she was dusting—I know how irresistible he is, any woman would want him to fuck her once she laid eyes on him. She claimed that she heard him call her name. Lying bitch! Marley told me that he had tried to hide in one of my panties but she had searched until she found him. He had told her that I had a sweet pussy and he didn't need hers, but the bitch knew that he couldn't resist a bit of ass. Anyway, I came home and found the house in the same mess that I'd left it in that morning. Marley had been fucking her ass *all* day. Boy, I beat that bitch until she was blue! If Marley hadn't stopped me I would have killed her!"

The fat bitch is delusional—she honestly thinks her dildo is a real man!

"Now I won't have a maid in my house unless she is

skinny—anorexic bitches don't do anything for Marley. Thankfully he hasn't fucked another woman since that horny, lying bitch made him fuck her ass. Occasionally I will let him dip the tip of his cock in my ass just to keep him happy. I try to do what I can to keep him satisfied, giving him pussy whenever he wants—which is *always*. Weekends I order take-away, lie in bed and let him fuck me. He is very jealous—I can't let him know other men fuck me. I have to sneak them into my spare room quietly."

She opened her eyes suddenly and smiled down at him. "Anyway, enough about me and my wonderful love life, do you want to talk about yours?"

"I-I am not dating anyone at the moment," Mason said with a slight stammer.

"Mason honey, you never date women. You fuck them and leave them."

"I've had steady girlfriends in the past," he lied, trying not to piss her off again.

"No, you haven't. But it doesn't matter to me. I am exactly the same—I rarely fuck the same guy twice."

You mean no guy would fuck you twice.

"All this talk about fucking has heated my blood. I am anxious to get my pussy on your big cock. Marley's the biggest cock I have ever had but yours looks a shade bigger and thicker. Let me get naked."

She started taking her clothes off—she was even fatter than he'd realized. She quickly pulled her bra off. Her breasts dropped about an inch but they were quite a decent pair and her prominent nipples looked like juicy, brown berries. He found himself wanting to taste them.

The G-string craze had made no impression on her—his fifty-one-year-old mother wouldn't be caught dead in the big white drawers Hailey was wearing. She rolled them down her massive thighs and kicked them aside. She didn't bother to trim her pubic hair or wax her bikini-line either. Environmentalist needn't worry about over-logging of the Brazilian rainforest—Hailey's forest could single-handedly prevent Global Warming. She cupped her breasts and said, "Take a look at a *real* woman, sugar. I am a work of art— God knew exactly what he was doing when he fashioned this body so I don't mess with his masterpiece."

She spread her legs slightly, parted the abundant hair and fingered her fat clit for a moment. "I refuse to shave my pussy so that men can act out their *paedophilic* tendencies. Why would a grown man want to fuck a woman whose pussy reminded him of a pubescent girl? I hope you aren't one of those men, Mason. If you are, check yourself, sugar."

She turned around slowly. "The cheeks of my ass love being together so I don't wear any knickers in the summer— it would be unkind to separate them even with the string of a thong. But now that it's winter I think it's cruel to leave them to freeze, so I keep them snug in comfy knickers. Women who 'freeze their butts off' in tiny underwear even when it is snowing should be fined for cruelty."

He got his first glimpse of her ass as she faced away from him. It was as fat and as dimpled as he'd imagined but for some unknown reason the thought of pushing his cock between her outsized cheeks made it rock hard again.

"You are *just* like Marley, you naughty boy!" she scolded as she turned to face him. She moved toward the bed and climbed on top of him, naked except for her glasses. "As soon as he sees my naked body he *has* to have me. If I forget to wear a bathrobe when I come out of the shower in the morning I have to climb back in bed for him to fuck me again before he lets me go to work."

She spread her pussy lips carefully before she sat on his cock. "I don't want my cunt hairs to cut your sweet cock, baby. Marley loves my hairy tush but it can be *lethal* to other men."

He groaned as her pussy enfolded his cock in a bear hug.

"You are definitely bigger and broader than Marley." She leaned over and kissed the undamaged side of his mouth. "It's a good thing I'm wet from the fucking he gave me earlier."

"You used a dildo when you knew I was coming over?" he asked indignantly, momentarily forgetting the peril he was in.

"Marley is more than a dildo, baby." She wriggled her fat hips and took the last inch of his cock inside her. "I have to leave him home now because of the frequent random searches they carry out at work. By the time I get home in the evening my pussy is drenched from thinking about him being *hard* all day waiting for my return. As soon as I walk in the door I jump in bed with him and we fuck for hours. Today being a Friday we would normally have been fucking now. I had to slip a sedative in his brandy earlier or he wouldn't have even let me answer the door. Like I said before—Marley hates interruptions when he's fucking me."

Unbelievable!

She lifted her breast and offered him her erect nipple.

"Don't even think of biting my nipple off!" she warned. "Remember I have *two* nipples—you only have *one* cock."

He opened his lips and sucked her nipple into his mouth. She pressed her breasts against his face, completely covering his nose and mouth. He panicked as she seemed unaware that she was suffocating him. He pulled desperately on the handcuffs as he struggled for breath. Finally, she pulled back slightly and he filled his lungs.

"Are you trying to fucking *kill* me?" he gasped.

"I am so sorry, sugar," she kissed the top of his head. "I get carried away whenever someone sucks on my nipples. It's the only thing that Marley can't do for me. I miss it."

She offered her nipple again. He took it more cautiously this time. "Don't be afraid to give it a good hard suck, sugar. I'll hold it this time so there'll be no danger of suffocation."

She raised herself and started to move up and down on his cock. He closed his eyes, sucking hard on her fat nipple as she rode him. For a big girl she was shockingly nimble of waist. With his eyes closed, blocking out the sight of her fat ugliness, the sex was amazing. Her pussy was hot and wet, yet it gripped him tightly.

He sucked on her nipple harder.

"That's right, sugar. Just keep sucking on my nipple as I fuck you." She deftly switched one big, hard nipple for the other and he latched on, enjoying the way it filled his mouth. Instantly she quickened her pace, fucking him furiously. "Harder, Mason sugar, harder! Bite it for me, baby, bite it!"

She came, her pussy squeezing his cock so hard he screamed as he came too, literally feeling the cum travel from deep within his balls and spurt up inside her. She rode him until his cock stopped twitching then collapsed against him, trapping his face between her sweet-smelling breasts, but this time she left him room to breathe.

"Sorry if I hurt your cock, Mason baby. I do special exercises to keep my pussy tight for Marley," she explained. "He likes a *very* tight pussy and I would die if he left me for a woman with a tighter pussy, so I spend all day at work secretly doing pussy aerobics."

She lay like a dead weight against him for a few minutes. Suddenly she seemed to stop breathing and his mind was filled with an image of her dying on top of him.

"You okay?" he asked frantically.

"I'm fine, sugar. I was just re-living the memory of your sweet cock inside me." She sat up and kissed it. He flinched. "It is so sweet I think I'll keep you handcuffed to this bed for the next week or two."

"Hailey, this has gone far enough! Release me NOW!"

I've never hit a woman but God help me, I'll punch this fat bitch!

"Keep your voice down, Mason. If Marley wakes up and hears you I'll be in trouble. He's threatened to leave me if I ever let another man fuck me. So keep talking loudly and I just might have to keep you here forever," she threatened.

"You can't keep me chained to the bed. What would happen when I needed the bathroom?"

Dopey cow hasn't thought the plan through.

"I have incontinence pants in every size—a medium should fit your trim waist. And don't worry about your bodily functions disgusting me. I did six months work-study as a nurse, I am used to things like that. Patients loved my sponge baths, especially the men. Don't worry about food either, I would feed you in the morning before I left for work and rush home every evening to give you your dinner on time. God, I hope nothing happens to me on my way to or from work...well, let's not worry about that. I've done this several times before and nothing happened. You'll be fine." She lay back down, put her head on his chest and curled herself into his body. "By the way, did I tell you that *Misery* is my favourite movie of all time? Personally, I think Kathy Bates was a little too soft."

The full horror of what she proposed suddenly hit him. He had to bite his lips to stop from crying for his mama.

"They'll miss me at the office," he said desperately.

"No, they won't, Mason darling. You are on leave for a month from Monday."

"My mother will miss me," he tried again.

"You would have been on safari when she and your dad get back from their Caribbean cruise next week. They won't miss you for another three weeks at least. When you don't call them from Kenya they will assume you are having too much fun to call."

"Hailey, I paid a lot of money for that trip. I can't get a refund at this late stage."

"Money's no object. My agency makes over a £1000 a night. I'll write you a cheque." She tweaked his nipple and asked nonchalantly, "Do you remember when Bertie went AWOL for a week last year?"

"Yes," he admitted, looking more and more traumatized by the second.

Bertie's wife had been frantic—his car had been found abandoned in Hackney. The police had suspected foul play but he had turned up unharmed a week later claiming that he'd had temporary amnesia. Later, he had bragged to the guys that he'd met a twenty-five-year-old Swedish tourist at a petrol station while filling his tank. She had struggled to open the cap to fill up her rented car and he had gone over to lend a hand. Afterwards, she had boldly told him that she'd always wanted to sample a Black dick. He had driven his car to Hackney, with her following in hers. When he had found the ideal spot to leave his car without fear of it being broken-into or vandalized, he had parked it, got into hers and they had driven to a hotel. He claimed that the two of them had fucked all week. The guys had been dubious— Bertie wasn't the kind of man a young, beautiful Swedish blonde *or* any other woman would look at and want to fuck, *unless* she was blind.

"He was here with me," Hailey lied. "As soon as Marley dropped to sleep each night I used to crawl into the spare room for the old fucker to suck on my nipples for the rest of the night. It's so wonderful to have someone sucking on your nipples when you fall asleep. The sucking action is so soothing it gives you the most pleasant dreams. Then to wake up the next morning to that wonderful pulling sensation—it's heaven! I had planned to keep him for two weeks but my nipples were so sore by the end of the first, I had to send him back home to his wife."

She rolled one of her nipples between her fingers. "I'll have to regulate your nipple-sucking because I wouldn't want to shorten your stay. I think half an hour each nipple, every night should be okay, don't you?"

"I can't suck on your breasts for a whole hour each night!" he protested.

"Mason, don't pretend that you don't like sucking a nipple. The way you wrapped your mouth around mine earlier told me that you didn't stop breast-feeding until you were eighteen months old. And even then you cried for your mother's nipples for another month," she declared with psychic accuracy.

She was a fucking witch!

Mason felt a chill run up his spine.

Lord, please let me see my mama one last time before I die, he prayed worriedly.

Hailey smiled. She could almost hear the wheels turning in his head. She'd overheard the guys talking about breast-feeding, competing for the dubious honour of being the one who had managed to suck his mama's titties the longest. George the BO king had won, claiming that he was still breast-feeding when he'd started secondary school at age eleven! Hailey had thought their conversation most indelicate. If she'd had access to their mothers' telephone numbers she would have taken great pleasure in calling every last one so that they could box their respective sons' ears.

The little display of psychic powers had frightened Mason—he should behave now. When she let him go he should head for the door and *not* for her.

Hailey loved the little 'Marley' story—she had made him sound so good she actually wished she really had a dildo like him. Maybe, it was worth a trip to Ann Summers to see if she could find one fitting his description. Her stories were becoming more outrageous and elaborate with each male colleague she suckered into coming over to her house. She should start writing them down—she could publish them in a collection of freaky short stories—like the book she had just read. Maybe she should contact the author so that the two of them could write a book together—call it *Bedtime Erotica for Freaks (like us)*.

Mason was eying her warily, like he expected her to suddenly break out singing, '*The hills are alive with the Sound of Music...*' Or slap him unconscious.

She had him exactly how she wanted him. Submissive.

A little more craziness should do the trick...just to make sure. She sat up and tilted her head, listening intently. "Did you hear something?"

"No."

"Shh!" She listened again. "You didn't hear that?"

"No," he repeated impatiently, still displaying the arrogance he seemed born with.

There was still a bit of fight in him, she admired his fighting spirit but didn't want to bear the brunt of it. Yes, a little more madness was definitely called for.

She tilted her head again and suddenly jumped off the bed.

"Shit! Marley's awake. He's calling my name. You have to go *now*." She started to unlock the handcuffs, muttering like a mental patient in Goodmayes Hospital, "Dear God, I hope he didn't hear your voice. If he knows that I've been in here fucking you it will be hell to pay. He's been threatening to fuck my ass if I misbehave. He'll do it tonight. I know he will! As soon as you are gone I'll have to quickly shower and give him some pussy. If I give him some pussy he might not suspect anything. Yes, as soon as you're gone I'll wash your cum out and give him some pussy."

Let me get out of this mad fucker's house before she goes completely insane.

Mason pulled on his shirt and trousers, stuffed his boxers and socks into his pocket and picked up his shoes. He was dressed in three seconds flat.

"Enjoy Kenya, Mason. If you don't see me at the office when you get back next month know that Marley has got me at home fucking my ass. He wants my ass *bad* and once he starts to fuck it, I know he won't stop. He'll fuck my ass *even* when I'm sleeping. I won't be able to sit down. I'll have to let my doctor sign me off work for the next six months or so. Hopefully, by then my ass would have gotten accustomed to the constant fucking."

"Take care of yourself, Hailey," he said as he edged away from her.

I hope Marley fucks your fat ass.

He caught himself.

Now she had him as crazy as she!

"Oh, Mason," she called as he rushed to his car barefooted. "You and I *really* should share that Player of the Century award."

One of the guys has been telling tales out of school, he fumed. *If I catch the fucker who has been leaking men's business to this fat cow, he's dead!*

"After all," Hailey continued, "I have fucked all of the guys in the office, including Mr Trotz whose lovely ass Marley helped me tear up in fine style." She inclined her head as if in deep thought. "I think that gives me a *slight* edge, don't you? Maybe we should let the guys decide."

He looked at her in horror—as all the others had done at the thought of anyone else knowing she had fucked them. Their reluctance to admit to the few hours they had spent in her bed perpetuated the myth of her virgin, unconquered status. She saw no reason to break the 'code of silence'. The company was rapidly expanding. There would be lots of new employees starting soon—lots of new men who would try to take her virginity.

"Don't worry, baby." She winked at Mason. "This will be *our* little *fucking* secret."

***

Poor Mason—competitive to a fault and lured by the idea of being the first. He was prepared to stick his dick in a woman he wouldn't have usually given the time of day. Poor baby, he will think twice about doing the same thing next time.

*****

EASY RIDERS

*D*affodil and Sunflower Gardner were so alike their parents had trouble telling them apart. It was highly likely that the twins had been mixed up as babies, that Sunflower could in fact be Daffodil and vice versa. Even scientists conducting twin studies of them and hundreds of identical siblings were staggered by their physical exactness. They shared the same taste in everything, including men. This caused the first fights they had ever had when they became teenagers but finally they came to an agreeable solution—sharing. Whoever met the guy first went on the first date, the other twin went on the second and so on.

When they decided it was time to lose their virginities they gave the matter serious thought. They wanted it done properly and by the same man; identical male twins would have been ideal but they knew none their age. They asked their friends who were no longer virgins for advice but weren't really impressed by their accounts. Finally they decided on Guy Eugene, the school's ex-sprint champion. He had been four years ahead of them and they had cheered wildly every time he crossed the finishing line but had never met him personally. He had been very popular and was rumoured to be a master at taking virginities. Less than a month after graduating university, he had opened his own fitness and leisure centre using the money he had earned advertising sportswear for a well-known designer. He was now hugely popular with the local women, anyone with a missing daughter, sister or girlfriend didn't have to look further than Guy's mansion.

But mere days before the twins approached Guy with their proposition, a young gynaecologist joined the local practice.

Dr Charles Wray had grown up privileged. He looked like a movie star, which wasn't surprising since his mother was a former supermodel and he'd inherited her great features. Most of the town's women immediately switched to his surgery and within a week he had a waiting list a mile long. Women suddenly needed monthly breast examinations and with the new awareness of nipple cancer many ensured that he checked their nipples thoroughly for any signs of this dreaded form of the disease. Some complained of aches in the vaginal region that necessitated him having to don surgical gloves and probe the area. Usually he diagnosed horniness and instructed them to have sex with their partners or husbands. Yet, they came back with the same complaint, time after time.

Mr and Mrs Gardener both agreed that none of the females in their family would switch to Charles's surgery. The twins pleaded with their mother when they caught her alone, trying to appeal to her romantic side but she adamantly refused to change her mind. She said it was unnatural for a young man to train as a gynaecologist, disturbing even.

The twins tried to book an appointment with him on the pretext of interviewing him for an article they wanted to write for the school's newspaper but his bulldog of a secretary literally threw them out on their ears.

So one Thursday evening they parked outside his home and waited for him, intercepting him as he headed for his front door after parking his gleaming Ferrari in the garage. He invited them inside for drinks and as soon as they had settled comfortably on his richly-upholstered settee, asked how he could help them.

They outlined the problem and why his help was vital in solving it. He was a little surprised by their request but immediately saw the benefits of having the job done by a professional, someone who *knew* a woman's body. He agreed to meet them at his surgery the following Saturday evening, saying that it was best to treat the matter as clinically as possible.

He was well-prepared when they arrived promptly at six. He had wheeled his partner's examining couch into his office, placed it side-by-side with his and signposted the girls' names on the wall behind.

"As you can see I have labelled the couches for ease of reference," he told them as they stripped as per his instructions. Naked, they climbed onto the couch and he hooked their feet into the stirrups in turn. "I will not get undressed nor will I allow myself to get aroused until the appropriate time. I will perform the removal of your hymens with strict adherence to medical procedure. I will arouse you both, then use my male instrument to remove one and then the other. Who is older?"

"I'm older by five minutes," Daffodil replied.

"Good, I will take yours first." He pulled a stopwatch from his pristine white overalls and handed it to Sunflower. "It should take me no more than a minute to successfully remove your sister's hymen but I will keep thrusting inside the vaginal receptacle for another two minutes or so to clear hymeneal debris. I will then take a minute or two to regain my composure before I proceed to remove yours. If timed with military precision, you would have both effectively lost your virginities at the same age."

"That's brilliant!" they agreed together. They hadn't given that aspect any thought but the doctor's plan would make the whole experience even more perfect. They had argued constantly since he had agreed to help them, each wanting to be the first but his solution was the most practical.

Charles moved to stand in the small space he'd left between the two couches, reached down and covered Daffodil's right breast and Sunflower's left with his hands.

"There are many erogenous zones on the female body, breasts are the most obvious because they protrude outwards and respond easily to touch. They can be aroused by fingers or by lips and tongue; the nipples can be licked gently, sucked firmly or even bitten. Breast sensitivity varies from woman to woman, a man should gauge a woman's reaction to his caresses to see what is suitable."

He tweaked their nipples and watched them both instantly harden. "Your nipples have both responded beautifully to my touch. Now I will draw them into my mouth and suck on them one after the other."

He bent his head and sucked on Sunflower's nipple. She moaned and writhed on the couch, unconsciously lifting her hips upwards. He let his teeth gently graze the hard bud as he continued to tweak Daffodil's nipple with his fingers. Then he switched sides and like her sister Daffodil's hips unconsciously lifted upwards seeking fulfilment.

"Identical responses," Charles commented as he finally raised his head. "I will now move on to what is considered the primary erogenous zone on a woman's body—the clitoris. Then to the insertion of my finger into the vaginal passage and the use of a series of thrusting motions that will parody the ones I will later employ when using my male instrument."

Although he had promised not to get aroused, the girls could clearly see the bulge of his erection showing through his overalls.

Charles placed his hands on the twins' vaginas and carefully stroked their clitoris to their very vocal enjoyment. Then he inserted his forefingers into their slick openings. "This is called digital penetration or more commonly finger-fucking."

"I will now free my male instrument and remove Daffodil's hymen." Charles slipped his rigid penis through the space between two buttons on his overalls. It was of average size with a granite-like consistency—perfect for effectively cutting through obstructing membrane. He positioned the head against Daffodil's vagina and commanded, "Sunflower, start the stopwatch."

Sunflower pressed the start button as Charles thrust forward, piercing her sister with surgical efficiency. Daffodil gave a little squeal but was soon lifting her hips to meet his deep thrusts.

"Doctor, your three minutes are up," Sunflower informed Charles but he kept thrusting and thrusting. In the end she had to shout loudly, "*DOCTOR!*"

"Sorry!" Charles apologized as he completed his last thrust and pulled his penis out of the warm, tight folds. "Even a doctor can get carried away by a tight vagina. That's why I took the precaution of giving you the stopwatch to time me rather than undertake the task myself."

He positioned himself between Sunflower's legs and as soon as she said, "Now" he used an identical forward thrust to remove her hymen as he had done her sister's.

***

An hour later they were sitting in his comfortable waiting room sipping chilled lemonade.

"Though you are not my patients I think it would be unethical for me to continue seeing you," Charles told them regretfully. "I have successfully treated the problem as you presented it to me, further treatments would be considered sexual intercourse."

The girls reluctantly left his office. After having dealt with their *problem* Charles's doctoral mask had slipped and he had fucked them with increasing vigour. Ridding himself of his overalls and pushing the two couches together so that he could plunge from one tight vagina to the other and back again, and back again.

***

Who should they sleep with next? Charles was bound by the Hippocratic Oath and would not reveal details of the treatment he had administered. After their wonderful experience with the gynaecologist, they wanted to also share their next lover but didn't want to be the subject of local gossip. The young men at college were notorious for bragging about their conquests and they had been queuing for the twins' favours like rabid beasts. Whoever was lucky enough to sleep with one or both of the Gardner twins would not remain silent about it. Any hint of scandal and their wealthy parents would lock them up and throw away the key.

It took two months for them to finally decide that Guy would be perfect. Most men hated his sexual prowess; he had neither male friends nor the need to brag.

It was easy enough for them to walk into his sprawling complex one Wednesday evening without arousing suspicion.

"Hi ladies, to what do I owe this pleasure?" he asked as he ushered them to the plush leather seats in front of his huge desk.

The twins looked at each other and then back at him.

"Are you thinking of joining?" he prompted as neither answered his question.

"Actually we wanted...," Sunflower began and then looked at her sister.

"...you to sleep with us," Daffodil finished.

"That wouldn't be a problem," Guy responded without missing a beat. At first they thought he hadn't heard them correctly, then he continued, "I have plans later but I am free tomorrow or Friday evening. Would you like my driver to collect you and bring you up to the mansion?"

"No," they replied in unison, then Daffodil continued, "we would prefer to meet you here at the sports complex Friday evening. That way we could pretend that we are here for a game of badminton or tennis without our parents getting suspicious."

"Great idea!" Guy agreed enthusiastically, then sobered as a thought hit him. "You are over sixteen, I take it?"

"We're eighteen!" Sunflower informed him indignantly.

"Good. I love pussy but I have worked too hard to build this empire to lose it *even* for twin pussy." He came around the desk and put his arms around their shoulders as they stood up to leave. "See you both on Friday."

***

Guy stepped out of his boxers and the twins gasped. He was easily twice the size of the goodly gynaecologist.

"You go first." Daffodil pushed her sister forward.

"No, you are older!" Sunflower retorted and gave her sister a push.

"Ladies, please don't fight over me," Guy teased as he advanced towards them, his stiff cock bobbing up and down with each step. "What's the problem?"

"You are bigger than the first man we slept with," Sunflower said as she eyed his cock warily. It seemed even bigger now that he was closer.

"Don't let this *little* thing worry you," Guy encouraged, stroking the very large thing. "He only looks fearsome but he is very gentle."

"We have changed our minds," Daffodil decided and reached for her discarded clothing. "Come along, Sunflower."

Guy moved past them and stood in front of the door.

"Girls, please don't leave," he implored. "At least give me a chance to tongue your sweet twin pussies."

"Is that all you'll do?" Sunflower asked uncertainly. "You promise?"

"I promise," Guy reassured her, breathing a sigh of relief. "I love to suck on a clit. I have been known to fall asleep with my head in a woman's crotch after *several* hours of clit-sucking. When I wake up I just continue where I'd left off until she tells me to stop."

The twins laughed and visibly relaxed.

Guy pulled on his dark blue silk boxers, took the twins by the hand and led them over to his large leather sofa.

He reached over and stroked Daffodil's clit as he covered Sunflower's with his lips. As soon as she came noisily minutes later he moved on to her sister. His fingers had brought Daffodil perilously close to orgasm herself, she came within minutes of him putting his lips on her clit.

"Now, you have confused me, whose pussy did I *just* take my lips off?" Guy laughed as he looked at them.

"Mine," Daffodil owned up reluctantly, she wouldn't have minded having another go before her sister.

"Okay, you can stroke my cock while I'm eating your sister." Guy freed it and placed it in Daffodil's soft hands. Lying back he winked up at Sunflower. "*You* come sit on my face."

Sunflower didn't need to be told twice, she straddled his head immediately. He positioned her pussy and tried to concentrate on tonguing her clit as Daffodil leaned forward and wrapped her lips around the head of his cock. He had enough experience to know that if left alone with a hard cock a woman would eventually jump on it of her own accord, he just needed patience and superb control. He was a master at controlling his body—years spent poised on the tips of his fingers and toes in the starting blocks awaiting the sound of the gun had given him phenomenal physical and mental control.

"I think I'm going to try it," Daffodil declared as she straightened and sat astride Guy's hips.

"I sensed you were the braver one," he commented, trying to incite their fierce sibling rivalry.

"She is not!" Sunflower denied, passionately. "I will try it too when she is done."

"That's what I like to see—young women who are not afraid to have a go," Guy praised, objective achieved.

He watched Daffodil carefully spread the lips of her pussy and place the head of his cock at her entrance. She made a few awkward attempts to sink onto it but didn't get the alignment quite right. There was nothing that he wanted more than to turn her onto her back and drive his hammer home but that wouldn't do in the present circumstances. Even if he was able to nail Daffodil, Sunflower would decline if her sister showed the slightest reaction of pain.

"Let me give you a hand," Guy suggested helpfully, rubbing his cock against her slick pussy before placing it against her entrance once more. "You licked him a little bit *too* dry. He will glide in smoothly now that his head is wet."

He held Daffodil's hips as she sank slowly onto him, making the tiniest adjustment of his hips as necessary.

"Is it painful?" Sunflower asked worriedly as she watched Guy's cock slowly disappear inside her sister.

"Not really," Daffodil responded in surprise. "It actually

feels nice."

"I told you girls he was gentle. You can bounce up and down on him if you want to, he won't mind at all," he encouraged. "Think of him as an exercise ball, the more you bounce, the more you work your thighs."

As a personal trainer, Guy knew the area most women complained about were their thighs. It was amazing the reaction he always got to the latter statement. Daffodil was no different to the hundreds of women he had made the comment to before, she immediately started to bounce more enthusiastically, a smile on her face.

"This is so much fun," she threw her head back and bounced even faster.

"I can't *wait* for my turn," Sunflower said jealously.

"Let me finish your sister off." Guy reached up and gently tweaked Daffodil's nipples. She gasped and stopped bouncing. He sat up and kissed her deeply, applying more pressure to her nipples until she started moving her hips in ever-increasing circles. Until she was pressing her pussy down against him, taking every last inch of his cock, her hip movements erratic. He eased the pressure of his fingers slightly before applying it again suddenly. Daffodil tensed, her whole body trembling for a few seconds before she came. Guy groaned as her pussy tightened on his cock. Taking a deep breath, he pulled her off slowly and laid her against the sofa.

"My turn, my turn," Sunflower said eagerly and pushed him back against the plush leather.

"Maybe I should be on top this time," Guy suggested. He wasn't sure if he could go through the agony of having another tight pussy slowly fit itself to his erect cock.

"No! I want the same as Daffodil!" Sunflower protested with a pout.

"Okay, come on then." Guy gritted his teeth and

prepared for the torture to begin again.

Shit! Had her sister been this tight?

It took all of Guy's willpower to smile encouragingly at Sunflower as she imitated her sister's earlier moves. Her pussy felt like a tight glove, squeezing his battered cock.

He had to make her cum quickly.

He sat up and stroked his thumb over her clit.

"No," she protested weakly, "I've got to bounce some more."

"You'll bounce all you want the next time, baby. I promise."

He turned her onto her back and continued to stroke her clit. As soon as he felt her start to cum, he buried his cock to the hilt and joined her with a few fast thrusts of his hips.

"The next time you will have the first ride," he promised Sunflower as he lowered his sated body onto hers.

***

Daffodil climbed onto Guy's face, positioning her clit against his lips as Sunflower climbed onto his cock. They had been doing this so often they could do it in their sleep. Guy now called them the *Easy Riders* because they had taken his comment about bouncing on his cock very seriously, testifying that their thighs had never been more toned. He had ensured that Sunflower had had the first ride on their second visit and they had alternated it with subsequent visits.

They had lost all fear of his hammer. Earlier they had teased it mercilessly, using both pairs of hands to stroke the shaft while passing the head from one mouth to the other and back again as Guy lay helplessly looking on. Just when he thought that he'd go quietly insane they had smiled at each other and climbed on top of him.

"I can't wait until Sunflower is done, I need something inside my pussy right away." Daffodil spread her pussy lips and demanded, "Tongue-fuck me *now*."

Guy smiled indulgently but obeyed immediately. They had come such a long way from the near-virginal young women who had walked into his sports complex four months ago.

Daffodil rotated her hips against his mouth and Sunflower synchronized her movements to match her sister's. Less than three minutes later they both came— exactly at the same time—a trick they had perfected within a couple of weeks of sleeping with him.

"Right ladies, you've had your fun. Now it's my turn."

Daffodil quickly knelt on the sofa and held on to the back of it as Guy positioned himself behind her. Sunflower took his cock in her hand and guided it into her sister's entrance. As Guy let the hammer slowly cruise its way into her warm depths, Sunflower wrapped her arms around him and held him tightly, pressing herself against him.

"I'm going to fuck you while you are fucking my sister," she declared, pressing her pussy against his ass.

"Is that your hard clit I can feel against my asshole?" Guy teased as he started thrusting in and out of Daffodil.

"Yes."

"Fuck me gently, honey," he implored. "I'm a virgin."

"You never had a clit up your ass before?"

"Never," he vowed. "So, please be gentle."

"Sorry, baby, I am going to tear your asshole up."

"Yes, Sunflower, show him no mercy!" Daffodil joined in the banter. "Give him the full length of your clit in his tight asshole."

These girls are so much fun, I'm really going to miss them, Guy thought sadly as he slowed his thrusts, leaned over Daffodil and stroked her clit with one hand as he reached back for Sunflower's with the other. Using the light, insistent touch they both liked he quickly brought them both to orgasm before spreading Daffodil's legs further apart and thrusting himself to a furious release. They all toppled onto his sofa and lay in a tangled mass of arms and legs before traipsing to his private Jacuzzi.

"Ladies, I have some bad news," he looked at them both with genuine regret. "This will be our last session."

"NO!" the twins shouted together. "Why?"

"My girlfriend's pregnant and I've asked her to marry me. She's said yes but told me that she will not tolerate my sleeping around." He looked at their disappointed faces and held out his arms. "Come now, don't be sad. We've had fun and were lucky that we've never been caught but all good things must come to an end some time."

"We're going to miss you so much." The twins moved closer and laid their heads against his broad shoulders.

"I will miss you too." Guy hugged them closer, kissing one and then the other. "What say we make our last ride a water ride."

"Yes!" Sunflower said eagerly and climbed on top of him, effortlessly finding his cock in the bubbling water and sinking on to it.

***

The twins knew that Guy would be a hard act to follow. The boys at college were so immature compared to him. In the end they bought matching Rampant Rabbit Thrusters and masturbated together but on their separate twin beds whenever they felt the need for release.

Then one afternoon while driving home from the cinema, they passed a large white van with the words, 'Jermain James – Landscape Gardener' written on the side.

"Pull over," Daffodil urged her sister, looking back in the direction from which they had come.

"What did you see?" Sunflower asked as she parked the car and pulled up the handbrake.

"There's a gorgeous guy in Mrs Malcolm's front yard,"

Daffodil told her excitedly.

"How do you know he's good looking?"

"I saw him."

"Daffy, I was doing 40 mph, how could you tell?" Sunflower asked, using the name she used for her sister *only* in private.

"Sunny, trust me, he was to-die-for," Daffodil replied, also using her sister's private nickname.

They walked back the short distance they had travelled, glancing over Mrs Malcolm's hedge at the shirtless Adonis laying the foundation for an elaborate water fountain. He looked up and caught them staring at him hungrily.

"Hi, ladies." He straightened to his full 6'1" and the twins gasped. He belonged on a runway *not* a garden walkway.

"Hi, Jermain," they chorused and secretly pinched each other.

"Ladies, you have an unfair advantage," Jermain sauntered up to the hedge, with a sexy hip swinging gait that almost made the twins drool.

"I'm Sunflower Gardener and this is my sister Daffodil."

"My hands are filthy." Instead of taking the slender hands extended to him over the hedge, Jermain laughed, shook his head and turned away. "By the way, ladies, nice try. Gardener—very funny!"

The twins stared after him in confusion.

"Daffodil and Sunflower! What are the two of you doing here? I haven't seen you in ages! My, look how you've grown!"

Shit! They had hoped the old biddy wouldn't be at home.

"Hi, Mrs Malcolm," the twins greeted their former primary school teacher with resigned smiles.

"Join me for tea and scones," she beckoned them before

calling to the chocolate Adonis, "Jermain, come and join us too."

"I'll wash up and be right with you, Mrs Malcolm," he promised before disappearing around the side of the house.

"Such a nice young man," Mrs Malcolm informed them as she poured Earl Grey tea into dainty China cups. "He was one of my brightest students before his parents moved away from the area. He and his brother were even worse than you too!"

"We weren't that bad." Jermain came through the front door, his magnificent chest now covered by a brilliant-white T-shirt.

"You were little terrors!" His former teacher smiled at him indulgently before remembering her manners. "Have you met my guests?"

"Yes." Jermain looked at them a little sheepishly. "Sorry about earlier...I thought you were pulling my leg."

"Why would you think that?" Daffodil asked.

"I'm a gardener...you are Gardeners. I thought you were little rich girls looking down your aristocratic noses at a mere workman."

"Ah!" The puzzled look they had both been wearing cleared as understanding sunk in.

"Don't pretend that you are a mere gardener," Mrs Malcolm scolded. "He is quite famous. The only reason I managed to get him to do my garden is because he's my godson. His designs have appeared in all the top magazines."

"Not all," he protested modestly.

"All the major ones," Mrs Malcolm asserted.

"What form are you girls in?" Jermain changed the subject, seeming embarrassed to talk about his achievements.

"Upper sixth," Daffodil informed him. "We go to university in September."

***

"Remember I saw him first," Daffodil reminded her twin as they walked back to their parked car after partaking as sparingly as was polite of Mrs Malcolm's Earl Grey tea, which they hated and her scones, which they thought were too fattening.

"You only saw him because I was driving!" Sunflower protested.

"It doesn't matter—I want him."

"That's not fair!"

"Mrs Malcolm said he has a brother, maybe you can have him," Daffodil consoled.

"He might not be as good-looking!" Sunflower retorted before pleading, "Daffy, please?"

"No, he's mine."

***

"Do you think we are doing the right thing?" Sunflower asked Daffodil as they crouched at the back of his van and waited for Jermain to finish work, a week later.

"Do *you* want to be invited in for tea and scones again?"

"No." Sunflower gave a theatrical shudder in response.

Mrs Malcolm had caught them twice again and subjected them to tea and scones when they had tried to have a chat with Jermain.

A minute later Jermain opened the back door of the vehicle to load his tools inside. The twins quickly lifted their fingers to their lips to indicate the need for silence. He smiled, closed the door and walked around to the front of the vehicle.

"Give my regards to your mother." They heard the sound of Mrs Malcolm planting two noisy kisses on Jermain's cheeks. "And thanks for doing such a great job on my garden."

"It was my pleasure." Jermain opened the door and slid

into the vehicle. "Just make sure that you water the plants as I have instructed."

Mrs Malcolm promised to do as directed and he started the vehicle. He drove around the corner and stopped. The twins quickly jumped out, hurried to the front and jumped in.

"What are you two doing in my vehicle? Running away from home?"

"Ha-ha, we are eighteen not eight," Sunflower informed him.

Jermain looked from one to the other waiting for an answer to his question.

"I want to cook you something special tonight," Daffodil invited.

"Just you?"

"Sunflower is joining us for dinner but she will make herself scarce afterwards," Daffodil declared ignoring her sister's gasp of disappointment.

"I could bring my brother along, maybe you—" Jermain started.

"No, thanks," Sunflower quickly interrupted. She didn't want the *ugly* brother.

"OK," Jermain agreed, seeming a little hurt by her lack of interest but he didn't press the matter. "Where can I drop you off?"

Daffodil gave him directions. Following them he turned right at the next corner and drove along the tree-lined street. They were home in less than five minutes.

"See you around eight then," Daffodil leaned over and kissed his cheek.

"Won't your parents object?" Jermain asked doubtfully as he eyed the large house and its immaculate gardens. The twins' parents were wealthier than he'd imagined.

"Dad left yesterday for a two-week conference in

Geneva and Mom went with him."

"OK. I'll come but I hope you can cook. After a hard day's work the last thing I need is indigestion."

"You don't have to worry about that, we can cook."

"I hope so."

"Mom's a chef," Daffodil reluctantly admitted. She had wanted to surprise him with a mouth-watering three-course meal.

"Great! I love to eat so make sure you cook extra."

"Do you think his love of eating extends to pussies?" Sunflower asked her sister as they watched him drive off.

"God, I hope so!" Daffodil replied fervently.

***

"His hands are empty, the mean bastard!" Sunflower observed, as she and Daffodil watched Jermain stride up their parents' driveway that evening.

She was happier than she had been earlier in the afternoon. Daffodil had promised to swap with her so that she could have a chance with Jermain as well. It wouldn't be the same as with Charles or Guy but it was better than nothing.

"Hi, ladies."

"Hi, Jermain."

"Which one of you is my date?" Jermain asked looking from one to the other.

"I am." Daffodil, wearing a red strapless dress, came forward and put her arms around his neck and kissed him.

Sunflower, wearing the exact style in black, looked on jealously.

"I hope dinner is ready," Jermain said as he slowly pulled his lips off Daffodil's. "I'm starving."

"We are starving too, we thought you'd never get here." Sunflower eagerly headed for the kitchen. "I'll serve it now."

"Sorry I'm so late," Jermain apologized as he pulled

Daffodil back into his arms. "I got caught in a traffic jam and barely made it home in time to shower and dress before heading back here."

Minutes later they were sitting around the table feasting on Chicken Cordon Bleu, served with asparagus and potatoes. Jermain had almost cleared his plate when he slapped his forehead in annoyance. "I forgot the wine in the car, I'll just go grab it."

He got to his feet and hurried to the door. Before opening it he turned and said, "The food's delicious. I'll have a second helping when I come back if you don't mind."

"No problem," Sunflower assured him as she exchanged an amused glance with her sister.

Jermain came back with a rather expensive bottle of wine, filled his plate to the brim again and attacked it with gusto. The twins watched him eat, silently asking themselves, *where the hell is he putting all that food?*

After cleaning his plate he stood up. "I completely forgot the roses I picked from my garden for you. I'll go and grab them."

"He is a forgetful *pig*," Sunflower whispered to her sister.

"Maybe he was just hungry," Daffodil covered her mouth to stifle her laughter.

"I don't think we should serve him desert," Sunflower decided. Their mother usually served mandarin oranges as dessert after the dish but they had used the fruits to make homemade ice cream instead. "It might make him too full to eat our pussies."

"*Stop it!*" Daffodil hissed, nudging her sister in the ribs and holding in her laughter as Jermain's returning footsteps echoed on the marble flooring.

A minute later he walked into the room with a bouquet of a dozen perfect roses in each hand.

"These are from your garden?" Daffodil asked

incredulously.

"I couldn't bring the best ones," Jermain apologized. "I'm keeping them for a competition next week."

"Jermain, they are beautiful," Sunflower accepted the offered bouquet and buried her nose in a fragrant rose. "Let me put them in some water."

"Come up to the bedroom," Daffodil handed her bouquet to her sister, put her arm through Jermain's and headed for the stairs.

"Are you sure you don't want to come too?" Jermain turned and looked back at Sunflower inquiringly. "I'd like to show you *both* my appreciation for the sumptuous meal you provided."

"Can you handle us both?" Sunflower queried, carelessly laying the bouquets on top of her mother's delicately embroidered tablecloth in her eagerness.

Jermain smiled as he put an arm around each twin. "Ladies, I'm a young man in the prime of my life—I could handle *triplets*—just lead me to the bedroom."

When they got to the room the twins shared although there were two guest rooms, he sat on the end of one of the twin beds and directed, "I want you girls to arouse me with a slow, sexy striptease."

Sunflower picked up a remote control, pressed a few buttons and soft, sultry music filled the room. Swaying to the beat, the twins slowly pulled their zips down, stepped out of their dresses and then their thongs in unison.

"Very nice," Jermain groaned, his cock like a rock by the time they had finished.

"Your turn now," Daffodil ordered.

The twins hugged each other and watched Jermain as he undressed. They waited with bated breaths as he pulled his boxers off. Not as big as Guy but almost. They turned and smiled at each other, then Sunflower leaned forward and tongued Daffodil's left nipple.

Jermain gasped in surprise. "You girls…?"

"Of course we don't," Daffodil retorted as Sunflower pulled her nipple into her mouth and sucked on it firmly. "That would be incest!"

"But you…," Jermain trailed off again, so aroused he had to bite his lip to stop himself cumming.

"It's just practical," Daffodil explained, as if it was the most natural thing in the world. "I can't reach my nipples so she sucks them for me, then I return the favour."

"That's *very* practical," Jermain agreed as he closed the gap between him and the girls. "So practical, I nearly came."

"You had better not be a premature-ejaculator," Sunflower warned. "You will need lots of stamina to satisfy us."

"Stamina is my middle name," Jermain assured her, kneeling between them and reaching up to fondle Sunflower's pussy as he put his mouth on Daffodil's.

***

Two and a half hours later, the twins seemed as though they were just getting started. Jermain was flat out on his back trying to recover from Sunflower's last ride. Daffodil took his deflating cock in her hands, intent on stroking it back to full alertness. They were too much for him—he needed help *but* it was in his car. Weakly, he sat up and reached for his boxers.

"I forgot—"

"*What* could you possibly have forgotten this time?" Sunflower demanded in exasperation. "Give me the car keys and I'll get it."

"It's too heavy for you to fetch. I'll go myself."

"We'll come with you," Daffodil offered.

"Girls, there is no need," Jermain protested.

"We are coming and that's final," Sunflower insisted.

The twins donned matching robes, hooked an arm through each of his and marched him down to the car.

"I think I've left my keys inside the house." Jermain searched his front pockets and came up empty-handed.

"They are in your back pocket," Daffodil announced, quickly fishing them out and opening the car door.

She screamed as the man, sitting with his face averted in sleep, suddenly awakened and instinctively turned to face her. She screamed again as she looked at him in confusion.

"Daffodil and Sunflower meet my brother Jeremy," Jermain said as his now wide-awake identical twin unfolded his length from the low-slung sports car.

The girls looked at each other and smiled in sudden understanding, then turned and looked at Jeremy hungrily.

"Hi, ladies. I see that you have exhausted my poor brother." Jeremy smiled sexily at them as he placed his arm around his brother's shoulders. "I hope you will now *exhaust* me."

***

I have a fascination with identical twins, as you may have realized from my story **Double The Trouble** *in* **Bedtime Erotica**. *This one is for the guys who share my fascination.*

*****

Naughty Professor

*G*raham Greene rushed out of his office, along the empty corridor and through the heavy entrance doors of the sixth form college where he taught Physics, to his parked Jaguar, designer briefcase in hand, his thoughts miles away—three and a quarter miles away, precisely. The distance between the college and Madame LaBelle's Exclusive Men's Club or Belle's Whorehouse as less sophisticated people referred to it. He was such a regular visitor there that he could do the journey blindfolded, using his cock like a homing pigeon to guide him straight to the abundance of young pussy—the house speciality.

Belle's girls were all under the age of twenty-five. As soon as they hit that magic age Belle retired them with a handsome payout. On retirement, a number of them married previous clients and became domestic goddesses; three had become doctors; seven now practised law; two had pooled their retirement lump sums and had created *Wicked Secrets,* an aptly named lingerie range. But Belle was proudest of her former girl who had gone on to direct and produce several bestselling porn flicks—three of which had cleaned up at the last Porn Oscars.

Belle herself had been forced into prostitution at the age

of sixteen by her father and her greedy stepmother when they'd needed a hit and couldn't pay their drug-dealer. It started with them offering her for drugs, then realizing the potential 'goldmine' they had right under their roof, it wasn't long before there was a steady stream of men coming over to the house to pay for a taste of her tender, young pussy. A few even sampled her tight ass. At seventeen she'd run away with a twenty-nine-year-old neighbour when he'd moved to Colchester to work. They had lived quite happily for eight months before he was killed in a car accident one evening on his way home from the office—most likely speeding in order to get back to his young pussy. Left with few options she had decided to go back on the game but on her terms.

Within a month she was sharing a flat with two other young working girls, within six she was renting a five-bedroom house and had officially become a madam. Now, eleven years later she owned the sprawling three-storey building she called home and had twenty girls in her employ. Her experience had taught her that men would pay over the odds for young pussy and ass. Using her natural business acumen she catered exclusively to this niche market—supplying where demand was greatest. She was aware that many of her clients would prefer even younger girls but she stuck to her minimum age requirement of eighteen.

The very first thing Belle taught her girls was that no matter how petite, they had the power to lead the tallest, strongest man by the nose—once he had a hard-on. The girls used that power in subtly different ways but no man left the establishment feeling that he hadn't received value for money.

The use of condoms was mandatory and the girls were regularly tested for AIDS. Belle didn't permit the use of drugs, she encouraged her girls to study, not to drink or smoke and to make full use of the multi-purpose gym and personal trainers on site. She kept an eye on all the girls while they worked from her high-tech viewing parlour. Any client foolish enough to rough up one of her girls found himself looking down the barrel of Belle's Cobra Derringer. Shocked at the speed of Belle's response, the clients usually dressed quickly and left without argument—if any had taken a moment to check the gun they would have found it unloaded and smelling of pussy. Belle was a voyeur *extraordinaire* and loved the feel of cold steel inside her as she watched the action.

Belle's girls were special—young, juicy but knowledgeable in the art of pleasure. Graham's cock jerked as he recalled his last visit and the choice morsel Belle had had waiting for him. The frisky Grenadian nymphomaniac-in-training, Marcia, was twenty but looked years younger. Not that he'd had any complaints—he liked them young.

"Professor Greene!"

He turned at the sound of his name and watched as Vivienne Chambers ran towards him, her large breasts bouncing unrestrained.

"Yes, Vivienne?" he asked impatiently. He was in a hurry to get home and have a rest before heading over to Belle's. His little Grenadian had exhausted him the last time; this time he intended to show her who was the boss.

"I didn't get a chance to prepare for the test you gave today."

"So, what do you want me to do about it?" He didn't hide his irritation. "You had a week's notice."

"If I fail another test my father will kill me!"

He doubted very much that the spoilt, rich girl's father would give her the spanking she deserved, much less murder the 'apple of his eye'.

"If you were so concerned why didn't you study?"

"I meant to but...Myles is so sweet."

"Who's Myles?"

"He is daddy's chauffeur. I sneak out late at night to meet him and it leaves me too tired to study."

"You're seeing your father's driver?" Graham asked incredulously. The girl stood to inherit her father's business empire and she was messing with his chauffeur!

"Well, not seeing exactly…more like screwing."

"As much as I would love to stay and discuss your *sweet* lover, classes are over and I would like to get on with my evening's entertainment."

"I can *entertain* you for the next hour while we discuss you giving me an A^+."

"What exactly are you suggesting?" he asked, not quite believing his ears.

"You have a PhD—I know you understand me, perfectly."

"You think you could sleep your way from an F to an A^+?"

"Professor, neither of us would be sleeping…trust me."

His semi-hard cock surged into poker-like rigidity but for once the rush of blood to his groin didn't fully shut down the function of his brain. She was like a stick of dynamite, one false move and her father's lawyers could have him thrown into jail before he could blink.

"Vivienne, go home and study. I will give you a make up test tomorrow."

"Graham, let's cut the bullshit and be honest with each other. I know you want me—I've seen you watching me. *And* what use will Physics be to me when I inherit my daddy's money or marry a rich man?"

"So why are you wasting time at college?"

"I'm humouring my father."

"Last year you were doing so well. What happened?"

"I discovered sex and I can't seem to think of anything

else. All I think about when I am not fucking is about *fucking*."

"This conversation is totally inappropriate. I suggest you pick up your books and prepare for the make up test."

Graham quickly opened his car door and slid onto the seat but not before she whispered, "I'll be at your house in half an hour. That should give you enough time to pick up any dirty drawers you have lying around."

She walked to her BMW convertible as he drove out of the parking lot. She was the only student allowed to park in the teachers' parking lot. She'd had her first car stolen from the students' parking lot only two months ago and no one had had the heart or the guts to make her move her car the first time she had parked in the more visible parking space.

Fifteen minutes later, just as he got indoors there was a tap on his door. He opened it to find her striking a pose, the hood of her coat pulled up over her head. As she brushed past him she said, "I was so horny I couldn't wait any longer."

He locked the door and turned.

His jaw almost became unhinged! She was standing in the middle of his living room, naked, her coat around her ankles. Even with his vast knowledge of gravity he couldn't understand how her breasts could stand out from her chest the way they did, with no visible means of support.

"They are marvellous aren't they?" She ran her hands slowly up her taut stomach and cupped them. She tweaked the nipples idly and they responded by puckering into pebble-hard points. "I inherited them from my mother—the only *good* thing the bitch gave me. My father met her in a strip club, you know. Instead of paying for a lap dance like other men, the fool married her."

"How can you talk about your mother in that way?"

"She is not my mother; she only gave birth to me.

Anyway, enough talk about her. She is probably fucking the new French chef as we speak." Holding his startled gaze she wet the fingers of one hand in her mouth, squatted slightly and slid them inside her pussy. "I hope you have a big cock, small cocks bore me to death."

"My cock is big enough for most women. If you've been fucking every man you meet and it has left your pussy slack that's your problem, don't blame my cock."

"My pussy isn't slack!" she retorted indignantly, pulling her fingers out.

"It might not be slack but it's definitely not tight. A minute ago I watched you push four fingers inside you without flinching, some women can't even take two or three."

"Look, are you going to fuck me or *insult* me? Your hour is nearly up!"

"You think an hour's fucking will get you an A⁺?"

"Professor, you're a man over thirty. Fucking me for more than an hour will probably kill you. Besides, I don't have time to waste—I have plans with Myles, later. So, *fuck* if you're fucking."

He would show her no mercy. She was young but she needed to be taught a lesson.

"I'm calling the shots here, not you!" he reminded her.

"So call them!" she pouted.

"I am going to try your *slack* pussy for size," he walked slowly over to her, "if it is not to my liking, I'll try your ass."

"Professor, I never thought you were *that* kind of man!" The surprise on her face shocked him. "Sorry to disappoint you, my ass is not on offer—I keep it for shitting only. It's pussy or nothing."

Mouthy little tease and doesn't take it up the ass! Damn!

He bent her over the back of his favourite chair with one hand, undoing his fly with the other.

"Cap that fucker before you put it in me—no glove, no fucking love!" She tried to rear up but he held her down firmly.

"I am capping it, just stay right there."

Did the horny bitch think that he would risk his life by riding her bareback? From all appearances she was more of a danger to his health than he was to hers.

He reached into the top drawer of his writing desk for the packet of condoms he had left there the last time his father's brand new young wife, Rebecca, had come by for an anal tune-up. At nineteen, she was thirty-eight years younger than her well-to-do husband. While his father had had to wait until the wedding night to finally get some pussy and still believed her story that he was only her second lover; Graham had been fucking her from the very night his father had introduced them, over dinner at an exclusive restaurant. Before the main course was served Graham had recognized the 'freak' in the girl and had slipped her his business card when his father had gone to the gents just before their coffees were served. His father had driven her home and kissed her goodnight at the front door as usual. She had entered her flat, walked straight to the telephone and called Graham, then taken a taxi over to his place. She had lived up to all his freaky expectations, the only woman he had ever met who seemed to prefer anal sex. He had spent several hours that night catering to her preference. People might condemn him but he felt that he was being a good son by helping the old man keep his wife happy—no point in her having an outside man when she could keep it in the family. Plus, the younger woman had made his father leave his mother after thirty-five years of marriage—he had to avenge his mother.

He admired Vivienne's smooth young ass as he rolled the condom on. Like most naturally big-breasted women she didn't have a prominent behind, but it was round and very firm. Such a sweet ass to waste!

"Hurry up and give me the cock! Tick-fucking-tock!" She wriggled her hips impatiently.

Her mouth was like a sewer. He would fill it if he didn't want to surprise her.

"Okay, *little girl*, time to rock and roll!" That was all the warning he gave her before he quickly spread her pussy lips and pushed his cock against her. He got the head inside but the broad shoulders gave some trouble.

"What the fuck have you got back there?" She reached back to touch his cock and he smiled as he watched her try to get her small hand around his big cock. She pushed him off and turned around to stare at him. "Professor, you should have told me that your mother had mated with a fucking horse."

"Don't insult my mother," he warned softly, stroking the offending member.

"That shit's not natural! Fuck the A^+!"

"Come on, sweetheart," he cajoled. "You said you like a big cock—I've got one, so enjoy it for the next fifty-five minutes."

Backing her onto his settee, he got on top of her and kissed her before moving down to her magnificent breasts. They were almost too perfect to be believed. She would be paid millions if she bared them for money. Pulling one of her nipples into his mouth, he tugged on it. She gave a moan and he looked up at her. She was watching him suck on her breast, her eyes half-closed, her mouth open in ecstasy. He tossed his head several times, like the horse she'd accused him of being, pulling the nipple sideways and upwards. She gasped and writhed beneath him.

"You like it rough, don't you?"

She didn't answer but when he moved to her other

breast she cupped his head eagerly. He tugged savagely, repeatedly, on her erect nipple and she gave a groan of pleasure with each pull of his lips.

Moving to one side, he slipped two fingers inside her. She was wet but he wasn't surprised to feel her pussy immediately hug his fingers; he had noticed her hand when she had reached back to touch his cock—she had extremely slender fingers. Her party piece was an act—a show of bravo by a girl trying to play the big bad hussy.

Slipping another finger inside her, he continued to finger-fuck her and maul her nipples until he sensed she was on the brink of cumming. Pulling his fingers out, he pushed her legs further apart with his knee.

She held his gaze defiantly, too proud to beg for leniency, but he sensed her trepidation. He kissed her as he positioned himself and slid inside her. Again the tapered head gave no trouble. He had to manoeuvre the shoulders but with a few shimmies of his hips he got them in too. The long shaft was more troublesome and he felt her tensing up.

"I am not going to hurt you, sweetheart. I will take my time and only give you as much as you can handle." He was content just getting his cock inside her. It didn't matter if he didn't get it all inside.

"I can handle it!"

The girl didn't know when to quit. For that she wouldn't leave until he had given her every last inch!

"And there I was holding back, thinking you couldn't!" He gave her another inch and felt her fingers dig into his shoulders. He ignored the pain, pulled back half an inch and pressed forward an inch. And so on, until he could go no further. "You're right, you *can* handle me. Now time to stir the coffee."

He stirred the coffee gently, alternatively kissing her or sucking hard on her nipples. She came twice within half an hour but he needed to teach the upstart a lesson. Plus, the clock on the wall told him that he still had another ten minutes—he may as well make use of them.

Biting her lip, she reached backwards and held tightly onto the armrest as he stirred the coffee more vigorously as he was about to cum. She gasped as he slammed into her and shot his load.

He tried to kiss her as he collapsed against her but she pushed at his chest. "Get off me! Your *fucking* hour is up!"

She slid off the settee, picked up her coat and slipped it on. Marching to the door, she turned and said, "Don't think that I am coming back here *every* time you give a fucking test! You've had enough pussy today to give me a pass for the next year!"

He had to admire the gall of the girl. She was trouble with a capital 'T', but what a sweet fuck she turned out to be!

His little Grenadian would have to wait a little longer, he needed all his energy reserves when he tackled her next.

***

Two weeks before the end of term.

Two weeks before he could pay midweekly visits to Belle's.

Two weeks before he could watch porn all night and sleep all—

"Professor Greene, I saw this perfect apple and thought of you," a soft voice interrupted his daydreaming.

He looked up at the young woman standing in front of his desk, her long, curly hair cornrowed into an intricate style, her white shirt tucked neatly into a pleated mini-skirt. A large shiny apple held in her outstretched hand.

His little Grenadian.

"Thank you, Marcia." He smiled as he took the offered fruit.

"You're welcome," she responded. She had the sexiest,

softest-looking pair of lips he'd ever seen in his life.

"Do you want to come to my house to watch a movie?"

"Yes, please," she agreed eagerly.

"Okay, meet me in the car park in five minutes. I can't be seen leaving the building with you."

"I'll be waiting." Smiling broadly, she turned and walked out the door.

After obtaining his doctorate Graham should have gone on to teach university students but the lure of younger, more nubile flesh had been too strong. Secondary school would have been his first choice but he hadn't dared take the chance—too much underaged, delectable flesh. Instead, he had applied for a job at the sixth form college, stating when questioned that he wanted to inspire young minds, help them reach their full potential. Except for the handful of gifted younger boys and girls, the students at the college were all over the age of consent, but he knew getting involved with any of them would be potentially hazardous to his reputation. Just being around them was enough and whenever he masturbated, he pictured one or more of his young students as he slowly stroked himself to a toe-curling release. When masturbation couldn't ease the throbbing in his loins he took a trip over to Madame LaBelle's and found the youngest-looking of her girls to satisfy his craving.

Although he had observed a number of his students whom he could have fucked with little or no persuasion, he had resisted temptation for four years. Fucking Vivienne had been a mistake of mammoth proportions. He had unleashed the beast inside him—he had to tame it or it would consume him.

He still couldn't believe that he had actually asked Belle to send Marcia over to his office in a taxi, dressed as a school girl. It was very risky but the thrill of pretending that he was taking one of his students home with him had overwhelmed his usual common sense.

He picked up his briefcase, locked his office and hurried to the car park.

Marcia was standing by his car, waiting eagerly. Her eyes lit up and she smiled as Graham approached. He quickly deactivated the car's alarm and got into the driver's seat as she slid onto the front passenger seat.

Let the games begin.

"Marcia, I am your teacher, it would be unethical for me to have a relationship with you."

"I can't help my feelings, professor. I love you so much. You don't have to make love to me. All I want to do is stroke your cock and give you a blowjob."

He looked at her soft lips and his cock hardened as he asked, "Do you know how to give a good blowjob?"

"I have never given head before but I know what to do."

"Haven't you been with another man before?"

"No."

"Are you telling me you are a virgin?"

Marcia didn't answer but blushed prettily.

Graham turned into the driveway of his three-bedroom house, opened his remote-controlled garage doors and parked his car in the roomy interior. Rather than walk back through the garage and use the front door as he usually did, he led Marcia through the emergency door which connected the house to the garage. He didn't want to risk anyone seeing a school girl visiting his home, even if it was a hooker dressed in school uniform.

"Would you like a Coke?"

"Thanks."

Opening his huge American-styled refrigerator Graham grabbed a chilled beer for himself and a Coke for Marcia. He handed her the drink and they walked side by side to his spacious living room.

"I'd love a place like this when I am a bit older."

"You'll need a handsome retirement from Belle to afford it."

If his parents hadn't paid for his tuition and given him the down payment for the house he would be living in a small one-bedroom flat somewhere, still paying back hefty student loans. He took a seat in his favourite chair, half-emptied the bottle of beer before leaning back. Marcia sat on the carpet beside the chair and slowly sipped her drink.

"Professor...?"

"Yes, Marcia?"

She looked at him knowingly, finished the drink with a toss of her head and got on her knees in front of him without waiting for his permission. She slid his zip down, reached carefully inside his boxers, wrapped her hand around his cock and freed it from captivity. Immediately it started swelling and acting the fool.

"I still can't get over how well-hung you are!" Her voice was full of awe as she stroked the stiffening length reverently. A slight inclination of the head was all the encouragement she needed to wrap her lips around the beautifully tapered head and draw the cock deep in her mouth with a heartfelt, "*Mmm*!"

Graham looked down approvingly as she carefully opened her throat and fed herself his cock. She gave good head for a girl who had just escaped the clutches of a strict, over-bearing mother. With a little instruction her beautiful lips could become weapons of penile destruction.

She looked up briefly, her thick-lashed eyes dazed with pleasure as she took a bit more of the shaft into her mouth. Graham cupped her head and encouraged, "Don't be afraid to take it even deeper—just open your throat and let it glide inside you."

Obligingly, she opened her throat and swallowed more

and more of his cock until her mouth was right up against his groin. He stroked her cheek tenderly in approval. "Well done, my sweet. Well done."

Graham had surprised himself by the restraint he had shown in 'breaking' Marcia. When she had arrived at Belle's the madam had immediately called him and informed him of her new acquisition. Marcia had been a virgin, for all intents and purposes, but had admitted the use of a foreign object to penetrate both her pussy and ass while self-pleasuring. Graham had immediately signalled his interest by booking exclusive rights to her for two weeks. These rights, of course, excluded Belle's instructional use of Marcia's charms. This usage didn't concern Graham, Belle was savvy enough to only utilize small implements, their sizes insignificant to Graham's cock.

Marcia, a freshman, had left for university as usual that morning, after having breakfast, her haversack slung over her shoulder. Her mother had had no reason to suspect that her daughter wouldn't be returning home that evening. However, if she had been a little more observant she would have noticed that the haversack was more rounded than usual—filled with clothes rather than hard-edged books.

Her mother's strict upbringing had exacerbated Marcia's highly-charged sexual nature. She had watched her daughter like a hawk, even periodically but discreetly checking her underwear for signs of vaginal or seminal discharge. Her ever-watchful presence had driven Marcia almost to screaming point, until she'd felt that she had to leave or do her mother grave bodily harm. All Marcia wanted was to be fucked fast and furiously. She had run to Belle's knowing that it would be the last place her mother would look and the ideal place to have her every sexual desire satisfied.

Graham had driven over to Belle's after work the same day and spent the first session simply enjoying Marcia's tight pussy. Belle had readied the younger woman for Graham's arrival with the use of her skilful tongue and a few fingers, bringing the girl close to climaxing several times but denying her the pleasure of release. Belle had slipped out of the room and left the naked, aroused young woman on the bed when Graham had pushed the door open. Marcia had shown no fear when he had stripped his clothes off and unveiled his rampant erection. He had lifted her slight body up in his arms and placed her onto the head of his cock. She had immediately wrapped her slim arms around his neck and sobbed the words, "Fuck me, fuck me", into his neck as he had held her slim hips firmly and quickly buried his thick cock to the hilt. Finding himself dangerously close to release he had pinned her to the wall and fucked her hard. She had welcomed the discomfort of his huge cock stretching her almost-virginal channel, cumming twice before he had shot his load. Drained, he had staggered backwards to the bed, still sheathed inside her. Without pause she had immediately started riding his hardening cock, the tightness of her pussy at odds with the wanton fire that seem to run through her veins. Belle had warned him in advance that Marcia was of a special kind but she had surpassed his expectations. Late that evening, he had walked slowly back to his car, so tired he'd had to leave the pleasure of her ass for the next occasion.

Which, thankfully, was right now. He reached down, lifted her mini skirt and encountered smooth, bare flesh. She was wearing a thong and her ass felt like silk. Graham fondled the firm cheeks for a moment before reaching for the tube of lubricant lying conveniently on his desk— another of the tools necessary for his stepmom's regular anal tune-up. He also needed it whenever he got the urge to masturbate and couldn't be bothered to move from his comfortable chair. He lubricated a finger and pushed it into

Marcia's butt, moving the string of the thong aside with his free hand. He expected a little more resistance than he encountered.

"Are you sure you haven't had a cock up this asshole before?" He asked adding a second finger.

"Yes," Marcia confirmed, groaning appreciatively as he pushed his fingers deeper. "I sometimes used a bottle neck while I lived at home but I've never—"

"A bottle neck?" Graham asked incredulously.

"My mother used to check my room regularly so I couldn't risk having a dildo in the house. A friend told me that bottle necks make very good substitutes, so I found a decent-sized bottle and used it as often as I could," Marcia admitted with a wink.

"You naughty girl." Graham smiled in relief—his would still be the first *real* cock in the girl's ass. "Let's go play some pool."

Marcia got to her feet, her eyes fixed on Graham's still exposed, erect cock which glistened with her saliva. He pushed the tube of lubricant and a couple of condoms into his trouser pocket before he swung her high up in his arms and headed for the pool room. Marcia wrapped one arm around his neck, buried her lips into his warm skin while she reached the other hand down and stroked his cock.

When they got to the den she reached out and turned the knob. He kicked the door open and walked over to the pool table. Sliding her out of his arms, he bent her over it, throwing up her skirt and baring her smooth butt to his eyes and hands.

"You'll never forget this game of pool. First, I am going to spank you for using that bottle neck. Then, I am going to open your tight *pocket* a bit more and stick my thick *cue* deep inside you." She gasped as he brought his large hand solidly down on the cheeks of her ass ten times in quick succession.

"Don't *ever* use that bottle again unless I say so."

"I won't!"

Her promise wasn't born of fear—the blows he administered were just painful enough to further heighten her arousal not seriously hurt her. He fondled her ass as he reached into his pocket for the lubricant. "Luckily you chose a slim bottle—it won't make much of a difference."

She reached back and wrapped her hand around Graham's erect cock. "No, it won't—your cock is so much fatter than the neck of the bottle."

"Yes, it is." Graham laughed softly as he liberally smeared the lubricant on two of his long fingers and pushed them slowly into her butt.

"I can't wait to feel a cock inside my ass at last!" Marcia moaned, momentarily lifting her head off the pool table.

"Patience! I need to break your tight rim a bit." He increased the thrust of his fingers until he was working them back and forth with great speed and force. "Damn, girl! You have the kind of tight ass that was made specially for fucking."

He squeezed a third finger inside her tightness and continued to finger-fuck her vigorously. Marcia came once as he fucked her digitally for almost five minutes, her asshole subtly relaxing and gradually widening as she hovered on the verge of cumming again.

"I think you're ready now." Graham pulled his fingers free, liking the 'popping' sound her ass made as it snapped shut. He quickly rolled a condom onto his cock, smeared some lubricant over it and rapidly stroked himself back to optimum hardness. "Spread your cheeks for me."

Marcia reached back, held the thong out of the way and spread her butt cheeks as Graham put his condom-encased cock-head against her. It was still a little tighter than he'd anticipated, as usual he'd underestimated the size of his own cock. He forced the rim open, using short stabbing motions, making small inroads with each thrust. Finally, the head was solidly lodged.

"Ready?" Graham asked the eager young woman who was rotating her hips, trying to impale herself back onto his cock.

"I've been ready forever, just fuck my ass, *please*!" she groaned.

He planted his feet firmly and proceeded to bury his cock into the hooker-in-training's backside. After several thrusts, he stopped to let his cock *soak* for a while. There was still a lot of ground to cover and he didn't want to cum just yet. She moaned softly when he slowly withdrew to plunge his *cue* a few millimetres deeper.

The last time Graham had fucked an asshole this tight he'd had to take his time and even then the young woman had begged him to stop every inch of the way. The girl had also been fresh at Madame LaBelle's and he had paid her extra for the privilege. The girl's own father had taken her virginity soon after her mother had left him for another woman, telling her outright that he wasn't paying for pussy when he had pussy under his own roof. The father had been fucking her regularly until a cousin of hers had told her how much money she was making at LaBelle's. The girl's father was a stingy, jealous bastard, so she'd decided if she was going to be fucked she may as well get paid for it. One night when her father was laid out exhausted post-fuck, she had packed her meagre belongings and split. Belle tried out every girl who walked through her door and it was to their benefit and edification—she taught them more tricks in a few days than they would have learned in a lifetime. So, the lady of the house, Belle, had had the very first piece of the girl's ass. She hadn't believed the girl's claim to a virginal asshole after hearing the story of her horny, incestuous father. When she found it to be true she had spent some time gently breaking the rim with a slim dildo, leaving just enough 'bite' for Graham, knowing his propensity for breaking-in sweet, young things. After paying the exorbitant sum that Belle had demanded he pay the girl, Graham hadn't backed down until nothing but his balls had been left outside. And it was a good thing too that he had enjoyed the tightness that night, by his next visit several men had also had a taste of the fresh ass and it hadn't been half as tight as that very first night. He had ensured that the same thing wouldn't happen again by booking Marcia for a full two weeks.

He held on to her hips as he buried his cock a few millimetres deeper every time he thrust forward. She had her hand on her clit, stroking herself as he fucked her. Her ass was nipping his cock with just the right amount of *nip* and the movement of her waist could only be described as 'poetry in motion'.

Minutes later as he quickened his pace, about to shoot his load, he was already forward-planning the work he needed to do to 'break' her tight ass over the weekend before sending her back to Belle's.

Slowly, reluctantly, he pulled his cock out of her.

"Let's go to my bedroom. I want to be comfortable as I fuck this sweet, tight asshole some more," he told her as he squeezed the smooth globes.

"Yes, please!" Marcia straightened off the pool table and turned around eagerly.

He quickly stripped her shirt and thong off. Her body was completely devoid of hair; her legs, pubis and armpits had all been waxed. Belle must have seen to it personally when he had instructed her to send Marcia over, dressed in school uniform.

Belle knew his tastes so well.

Marcia's breasts were small, almost childish and

Graham's cock hardened instantly as he looked at them. The sight of her slim body still did crazy things to his equilibrium.

He led her to his bedroom and pushed her onto the bed before ridding himself of his clothes. When he joined her she snuggled her head into his chest. Feeling surprisingly tender, he raised her head and kissed her. Her soft, full lips opened under his and he plunged his tongue deep inside her mouth, savouring her sweetness. She moaned in appreciation as he ran his hand over her chest and tweaked her nipples. Lowering his head, he sucked on the small erect buds as he snaked his arm around her narrow waist and fondled her butt before sliding two fingers inside her ass again. He spent a few minutes sucking on her nipples and finger-fucking her asshole as she stroked his cock firmly. When it felt fit to burst, he eased it slowly from her grasp, pulled his fingers out and knelt on the bed.

"Time to get back to fucking your ass, my sweet."

Marcia rolled a condom on to his thick length while he squeezed a good dollop of lubricant on her puffy anus and worked it inside with his fingers, groaning appreciatively as the rim gripped them. He placed her legs onto his broad shoulders and slowly pushed the head of his cock inside her tight rim again as he lowered his body onto her tiny frame. She groaned aloud.

"You probably had enough for one day," he commented as he stilled for a moment after once again lodging the head of his cock.

"No!" she denied as she started to rotate her waist.

"Don't worry. I'm only just getting started." Graham leaned forward and kissed her as he started to thrust. "Even if your ass is a bit sore I won't stop until *I'm* satisfied."

"Oh God, yes!"

Graham raised his body, balancing himself on his toes and kept up his short thrusts. When he sensed she'd had enough of being bent double, he sat back on his heels, lifted her hips and continued.

"You feel so good in my ass!" she sighed as she clutched the black silk sheets on his bed.

"I've just been teasing you with a little more than the head of my cock but I think you are ready for the full length now. Turn over and let me *really* fuck you," he instructed. She did so carefully, without dislodging his cock. She gasped aloud as he bent over her and plugged her with another inch. "Be brave, my sweet, I have several inches still to give you."

"I want them all!" she gasped greedily, groaning as he slid yet another piece of his rigid cock into her.

"You will have every inch," he promised and slowly buried himself inside her, penetrating inch after inch as she gasped and writhed under him.

Buried to the hilt, Graham paused to absorb the impact of her tightness before he kissed the side of her face and whispered, "You have taken the full length of my cue, my sweet. Now, I'm going to take long, deep shoots at your tight pocket."

"Please...please," she begged as she turned her head and offered her lips.

Covering them with his, he started moving backwards and forwards, swallowing her moans as he quickened his pace. As she relaxed he plunged his cock inwards with a bit more ease. Finally, he pulled his lips away and groaned, "I could fuck you all night!"

"I'm yours until Thursday, professor. Yours to do whatever you will," Marcia reminded him, grinding herself back against him as he thrust forward.

"Just make sure that no one else touches your sweet ass."

He would take her back to Belle's late Sunday evening— he knew himself well enough to know that he couldn't regulate his pleasures. If she was under his roof, he would completely exhaust himself by the end of the week. He wasn't worried about her trying to make a little extra; she was motivated by sex not money. Belle would keep an eye on her for him but there was still a chance that Marcia could sneak into an area not under surveillance by the CCTV with one of the other young prostitutes. Unlike Belle, the other hooker wouldn't use a moderate dildo to fuck Marcia, especially if she herself requested something substantial. He would be furious if he found her asshole not as tight as he had left it when he fucked her next.

He dismissed the dismal thought as he continued fucking her for several minutes, each thrust driving him crazier than the one before as her tight ass massaged the full length of his cock with strong, muscular contractions. The friction became so maddening as he neared his climax that he bit down on her shoulder to keep from screaming. When he shot his load he collapsed onto the bed, his cock still squeezed inside her. She snuggled back against him, purring contently. He wrapped his arm around her and held her for a while.

"You have *such* a beautiful ass. I'll definitely come around to Belle's for another piece of it before Friday."

Graham dropped off briefly and awoke to find Marcia's hand around his hard-again cock. Although the thought of plunging his cock once more into her ass appealed to him greatly, he resisted the urge. There would be enough time over the weekend to 'break' her ass fully, the more time he allowed in between the breakings, the more resistance it would put up.

"Get dressed for me again," he instructed as he swung his legs off the bed. "I'll wash my cock and you can practise your blowjob technique some more."

After thoroughly washing his cock in the large basin in his custom-built bathroom, Graham lay propped up on his side, idly finger-fucking her ass with one finger as he watched her deep-throat him. When the naughty professor finally shot his load, the eager school-uniform-wearing hooker drank every last drop.

***

Wednesday evening Graham heard a muffled sound as he headed for the exit. Curious, he went to investigate—it was after 6pm, the classroom should have been empty. He pushed the door quietly inwards and smiled as he watched the two eighteen year-olds engage in heavy-petting. The girl's shirt was open, the boy's lips wrapped around one of her breasts, covering the entire tip and sucking greedily. Her left leg was up on a chair giving him unlimited access so that his hand could freely move backwards and forwards under her skirt as he finger-fucked her. His stiff cock was gripped tightly in her hand as she jerked him off.

Graham stood watching them until she looked up—her eyes glazed with pleasure and saw him standing at the door. She gave a little scream, swung her leg off the chair and quickly turned aside to re-button her shirt. Her young partner was so lost in pleasure it took him almost a minute longer to catch himself and push his still erect cock back into his fly.

"Mr Braithwaite, this is no way to treat a young lady!" Graham admonished.

"I'm sorry, sir!"

"Run along home now," Graham instructed the embarrassed young man. "I will see Miss Matthews home safely."

Paul rushed out of the room leaving the frightened Cassandra at Graham's mercy.

"Get your bag and let me give you a lift home," he ordered the trembling girl, openly admiring the outline of the aroused nipple Paul had been sucking, through her shirt.

She quickly grabbed her bag and preceded him from the classroom, her head bent in mortification. He gallantly opened the car door for her and she slid nervously onto the front passenger seat. His cock was hard before he turned the key in the ignition. As soon as he pulled out of the parking lot, he turned to her and said, "I interrupted the two of you before you had a chance to cum. Take off your panties and spread your legs for me. I'll finish the job the young pup started."

She slipped her panties off and opened her legs slightly, nervously, like the young virgin she was.

"Wider," he commanded. "You didn't seem to have a problem spreading them for young Paul."

She moved them further apart. Not as far as he would have liked but enough for him to get his hand between her firm thighs. Her pussy was still wet and he stroked her swollen clit until they came to a set of traffic lights. He briefly took his hand off the steering wheel to lift her leg slightly so that he could slip one long finger inside her tight pussy. As promised he continued the finger-fucking that Paul had started as they cruised along the deserted streets.

She glanced nervously around her every time they passed the occasional pedestrian or car.

"The windows are tinted—no one can see what we are doing."

Immediately she opened her legs wider and tilted her pussy up towards his hand. If he had known the *shy* little thing was more concerned with being seen than being fingered he would have told her that as soon as she had entered the car, though he'd expected her to notice that the windows were darker than usual.

It was awkward using his left hand, trying to stroke her clit and increase the tempo of his thrusting finger, but he did his best and soon she was moaning. She reached down and covered his hand with hers, thrusting his finger deeper and faster into her pussy than he'd been doing. She was a live wire! He'd suspected that there might be a healthy sexual appetite lurking under her virginal exterior but he had underestimated it. She groaned loudly as she came seconds later.

"Did you let young Paul fuck you as well?" The question was purely academic, he didn't think that she'd ever had anything larger than a finger in her pussy but with these tight, young girls one could never tell.

"No, professor."

"Are you a virgin?"

"Yes."

"I think you are lying to me. You feel like you've had a cock inside you before."

"No, I swear Paul has only put his fingers inside me."

"I think he put his cock inside you and you liked it."

"No, I don't want to get pregnant."

"You could have used condoms."

"They are not 100% safe. My friend and her boyfriend used condoms but she got pregnant anyway, now she can't go to university. My parents would *kill* me if that happened to me."

"Would you have sex if there was no risk?"

"Maybe…I am not sure. But there is no foolproof method."

"What if I told you that you won't get pregnant if I made love to you?"

"I won't believe you!"

"It's true. I had a vasectomy five years ago. I am as harmless as a fly!"

Graham had no desire to be a father and didn't want any woman saying 'oops!' if a condom burst. He mightn't have minded having a son but the thought of a grown man eyeing *his* young daughter the way he looked at young girls turned his stomach. Worse was not knowing if he could trust himself around a nubile young female—even if she was his daughter. Every Christmas having his brother's two young teenaged daughters jump all over him in their eagerness to embrace their only but favourite uncle when he visited for the holidays was exquisite torture. He knew he could fuck either or both of them if given half a chance. He also knew that his older brother would slice his cock and balls off, and feed them to him before leaving him to slowly bleed to death if he ever messed with his daughters.

"But Paul's my boy—" Cassandra started to protest.

"Paul's exactly that...a boy!" he interrupted. "Do you think I would have run away and left you the way he did earlier?"

"I don't know."

"I wouldn't have."

"He was probably scared." She defended her boyfriend of two years.

"Exactly, he ran like a scared little *boy* and left you. A man, like me, would have stood by your side and faced the problem head on."

He could see her digesting his words. He would let her ruminate on them for the next two days. "I'll take you home now but come to my office after classes on Friday and I'll show you the difference between a man and a boy."

He pressed the accelerator and the car responded smoothly. Five minutes later he pulled up to the kerb, two corners away from her parents' home.

"Until Friday," he whispered as he quickly slipped his hand under her skirt and stroked her clit. Just when he felt her hips begin to move to the rhythm of his caressing fingers, he withdrew his hand.

Leave her hungry.

"Friday." He straightened and turned the key in the ignition, indicating that he was finished with her for the day.

"Friday," she repeated and slipped out of the car.

Two days to wait! Too long! Thank God for his sweet little Grenadian.

***

The tap on the door of his office was so soft if he hadn't been expecting it, the sound would have escaped his notice.

"Come in," he shouted, folding away the Friday edition of The Times newspaper and turning off the reading lamp. Soft light filtered through the windows, the lack of artificial light giving the room a cosy, intimate atmosphere.

Cassandra entered the room, head lowered and stood just inside the doorway.

"Lock the door and come over here to me, sweetheart."

She fumbled with the lock, her nervous fingers turning the simple task into a complex operation. Finally after three tries she managed to slide the security latch downwards before she turned and walked slowly to the front of his desk.

"Closer, honey," he urged, his penis already throbbing at the sight of her young breasts straining against the material of her shirt.

She moved around the desk, her steps becoming slower the nearer she got to him. Finally, she was close enough—he suddenly reached out a long, muscular arm and jerked her forward onto his lap. She gasped, her eyes coming up to meet his briefly before she lowered her head again.

"Don't be afraid of me. I could have told your parents what I'd witnessed between you and young Braithwaite but I didn't. Why do you think that is?"

"I don't know."

"You are a very beautiful girl. I like you a lot and wouldn't want to see you get into any trouble." He kissed her softly. "I was once your age and I understand how it feels to have all those hormones running through your body. Wanting to have sex but your parents telling you it's wrong…wanting to have sex but afraid of getting pregnant…wanting to have sex but afraid the boy you gave your virginity to would lose respect for you."

"That's *exactly* how I feel," she raised her amber gaze to his in surprise.

"I would respect you if you gave your virginity to me. I would treat it like a precious jewel and treasure the memory for the rest of my life." He kissed her more deeply this time, cupping her breast and tweaking her nipples through her clothes. "Losing your virginity can be *very* painful if it isn't done right. Young Paul would make a mess of it but I have lots of experience, I would cause you only *pleasurable* pain."

"But you're older. We couldn't get married if—"

"I told you that I can't get you pregnant." He opened his top drawer and pulled out two sheets of folded paper. "Here's the proof—the date I had my vasectomy, the surgeon who performed the operation and the hospital where he performed it. I am also going to use a condom so you don't have to worry about catching any diseases."

"You make it sound so…" her voice trailed off as he found her clit and massaged it through her panties.

"…wonderful," he finished as he slipped the gusset aside and touched her springy pubic hairs lightly before running his fingers between the lips of her pussy. She was already moist.

It was so easy to arouse these sweet young virgins.

He opened the slick folds and massaged her clitoris firmly. Weakly she tried to snap her legs together, but he increased the pressure briefly on both her nipple and her clit. She gasped and surrendered, moving her hips in time with the stroke of his fingers. He pushed a finger inside her, pulled it out slowly, then thrust it deep a couple of times before he said, "Think of my cock doing the same thing my finger is doing right now. Imagine something bigger than my finger sliding even deeper inside you as I suck on your nipples."

"How much bigger?"

"A little bigger but don't worry I will take my time. I wouldn't give you more than you can handle." He smiled as he remembered saying the same words to Vivienne.

"I am not sure that I can handle anything that big!"

"Trust me, sweetheart, you are a tall girl—your pussy's nice and deep, you will be able to handle my cock quite easily. I'll start you slowly, one finger, then two—next you'll be ready for my cock." He pulled his finger out and moved his hand off her breast. She gave an involuntary sound of protest but he deliberately ignored it. "Let's have a drink and get more comfortable with each other."

Slipping an arm around her small waist, he swivelled his executive black leather chair around to face his skilfully concealed mini-bar. One-handed he retrieved two glasses, a dozen or so ice cubes and a bottle of cream liqueur. He poured the light creamy liquid over the ice-cubes and then used a stirrer to vigorously chill the liquid with such amazing dexterity that none of the liquid was spilled although the glass was nearly full. "I used to work in a bar part-time during my college days," he explained, seeing her look of astonishment. "Have a sip."

"I don't really drink."

"Just have a small sip, you are going to love it, trust me."

With her face clearly showing that she didn't believe him, she took a sip and then smiled as she took the glass from him. "It's delicious!"

She took a generous mouthful. And then another.

He tweaked her nipples through her shirt and she wriggled provocatively in his lap.

"Do you want some?" she asked offering the frosted glass to him.

"No, you finish it. I'll pour myself a brandy." He placed two ice cubes in a tumbler and poured a small measure of Remy Martin over it.

"I can't believe how lovely this is," Cassie remarked as she took yet another sip.

"I have it sent specially from Guyana." He tossed the contents of his drink back, loudly crunching the half-melted ice cubes as he placed the glass on the polished surface of his desk. Slipping the gusset of her panty aside, he slid his finger back inside her. "Now let's get back to those fingers—I think you're ready for another one. Open wider for me, sweetness."

She raised herself slightly and spread her knees, then whimpered softly as he squeezed another finger into her tightness.

"Two fingers give double the pleasure of one," he promised as he stroked her clitoris with his thumb and kept his fingers just inside her entrance.

As soon as she relaxed, he started a slight circular motion with his fingers. Her hips followed the movement in a counter-rhythm, unconsciously helping to widen the opening of her passage.

She started giggling and he knew the 40% by volume liqueur was creeping up on her without warning. The drink was perfect for seduction, its creamy flavour masked its alcohol content. He had successfully used it many times to wear down the defences of less than willing young women.

"See how easily two fingers fit inside your pussy? Soon you'll be ready for my cock." He held her skirt out of the way so that she could watch as he thrust the tips of his fingers into her pussy in short jabs. He let the hem of the skirt fall back in place after a while. Immediately, she gathered the material in her hand and held it so that she had a clear view. He opened her pussy lips with his free hand and kept plunging his fingers back and forth. Her eyes never wavered from the sight as she kept sipping the liqueur. A soft mushy, squishy sound filled the quiet room and even in the fading light the moisture on his fingers was clearly visible. "Your pussy is already wet but I am going to suck on your nipples and make it even wetter. My cock will *just* slip inside you later."

He slid his fingers under the buttons of her white shirt, skilfully undoing them one-handed. Her cotton bra was a cup size too small and her round firm breasts strained against the material which cut into their brown flesh. He eased his fingers under the cotton and tweaked her nipple between thumb and forefinger, it hardened instantly.

"Bare your breast for me. Let me tongue your sweet little black button nipples."

Eagerly she drained the glass and placed it on his desk, then pushed the cup of her bra downwards, oblivious to the faint sound of ripping as she revealed her pert breast. He covered her dark nipple with his mouth and her moans soon filled the room, making his cock hardened to bursting in his boxers. He released her nipple to catch his equilibrium, opening his fly to give his cock room to breathe. Her nipple became even more puckered as the AC hit it. He ran his tongue wetly around the areola and sat back to let the cold air freeze the moisture. She gasped and instinctively brought her hand up to cover the pebble-hard tip but he stopped the movement and covered it instead with his lips, drawing the swollen bud deep into the wet heat of his mouth and sucking firmly. She convulsed, dropping her head weakly onto his as he ravished her distended flesh. He freed its twin, which was already erect and transferred his lips to it as his fingers massaged the other saliva-drenched bud firmly. The restriction of her bra was hampering his access, so he pushed her back gently against his desk and once again reluctantly released her nipple.

"Don't stop...suck it...suck it," she implored cupping her breast with one hand and the back of his head with the other, trying to bring nipple and mouth together but misjudging slightly in her inebriated state. Her face was flushed, her eyes closed, her swollen lips parted.

"Let me take your bra off, honey." He leaned forward and teased her nipple with his teeth as he quickly slipped her shirt and bra off. He then slipped her panties off and swung her legs over so that she was now sitting astride his powerful thighs, wearing only her skirt. He pulled her crotch onto his silk-covered bulge and rubbed himself against her.

"Feel that, sweetheart?" She nodded a little drunkenly. "If you are a *very* good girl, I'll give you a piece of it before you leave here this evening."

"It feels big!"

A little more alcohol? Perhaps not. He couldn't risk her going home drunk to her parents.

He took the weight of her breasts in his hands and pushed them as close as possible together so that he could run his tongue over their taut peaks with just a slight sideways movement of his head. She pressed harder against the bulge of his cock and wriggled provocatively as he kept sucking on her breasts. He would definitely shoot his load if she continued at this rate.

Knowing that he couldn't easily get the head of his cock inside her without some more careful preparation, he swung her legs to the side to continue the fingering, squeezing his fingers back inside her.

"Yes, push your fingers inside me again," she moaned as she watched him thrust them back and forth a few times.

"Do you like them?"

"Oh yes! They hurt a little bit though."

"Pleasure is always a little painful."

"I don't really mind the pain."

"Good, because my cock is going to hurt at first but it will give you so much pleasure afterwards you will be glad that you didn't let a little pain stop you."

"Okay."

He kissed her, pushing his tongue deep into her mouth as he carefully deepened the thrust of his fingers. Ripping her hymen was a pleasure he wanted to reserve for his cock, so he didn't risk burying them too hard or too deep. He almost couldn't wait until he got her pussy to the stage where he could slide three of his long fingers inside her. There was nothing like finger-fucking a tight pussy—*well*, except for fucking it. For a few moments he kissed her, rolled her nipple and stroked her clit as he prepared her for the final hurdle.

"Good girl, you are as brave as a lioness," he praised as he broke the kiss.

"Are you going to make me cum like you did in the car?"

"Yes, but I will use my cock not my fingers, you will enjoy it so much more."

So far he'd deliberately stopped each time he felt her getting ready to cum. He knew she might be capable of having one orgasm after the other—she had demonstrated the possibility in his car but he didn't want to take any chances, that evening might have been a one-off. "Are you ready?"

She nodded.

He set her on her feet as he stood up and stepped out of his trousers. He had hoped to slip his cock to her before she caught sight of it, but it wasn't to be. He left his boxers on—he'd pull his cock through the opening and keep part of it hidden. He sat back in the chair, reached in his drawer for a condom and pulled her onto his knees.

"Remember I'm only giving you a small piece today, so don't be afraid," he reminded her as he pulled it out, trying to keep at least a quarter of it inside the boxers. But the snake reared its damn head and revealed its entire length. The fucking thing had a mind of its own!

Cassandra gasped, jumped up and covered her eyes. "NO!"

"Sweetheart, I *won't* force it inside you. I'll let you sit on it and take as little or as much as you want."

"I can't get *that* inside me!"

"Look how small the head is—no bigger than my two fingers and remember how nice they felt inside you."

"The head of your penis is bigger!"

"It's not. Trust me. I've had girlfriends who were virgins and once I got two fingers inside them the head slipped inside them quite easily."

"Are you sure?"

He could sense her weakening—time for the *pièce de résistance*—the black condom. He slipped it on quickly and watched his cock instantly look smaller.

Good old black—so slimming!

She moved a little closer and touched it.

"Yes, stroke it just like that," he encouraged, wrapping his hand around hers and moving it up and down. "See how nice and smooth it feels. It will slip inside you so smoothly you will hardly notice it's there."

She still looked uncertain.

"Cassie, honey, I am doing this for your sake more than mine. I could go home and masturbate but I want to give you a taste of heaven. Show you what other girls your age have been enjoying since they were thirteen or fourteen years old."

"Thirteen or fourteen…?"

"Sweetheart, you must be the last virgin standing. All your friends have been getting their groove on and probably laughing at you behind your back."

He watched several emotions quickly flit across her brow.

"Let me suck on these buttons while you decide." He leaned forward and sucked her nipple into his mouth. He sat back, still hanging on to the nipple, pulling her closer. She straddled his knees. And still he leaned backwards, pulling painfully on her nipple—moving her closer to the snake—within striking distance.

"Just try a tiny piece and see if you like it." He lifted her up and settled her entrance on the head of the snake. "If you don't, I'll make you cum like I did in the car and then take you home."

She hung on around his neck for dear life as he relaxed his biceps and let the weight of her body ease her down onto the cobra. His snake had been hard for so long without relief it was beginning to ache but it could bear anything at the moment. Her tight pussy closed over the head but she jumped up as soon as she felt the first bite. Thankfully, she didn't jump too far; she just lowered her legs to the floor and stood over it.

"Sit on it again, honey," he encouraged as he cupped her breasts in his hands and pulled a nipple into his mouth. If she did the deed herself she would resent him less, afterwards. He worked on the erect buds of her nipples in earnest. He had been teasing them lightly before but now he gave them his full attention, pulling hard on each of them in turn. She lowered herself and he used his teeth to craze her nipples just painfully enough to distract her as the head slipped inside her. She gave a little scream, the alcohol numbing but not completely masking the pain, as the barrier of her hymen finally gave way. He reached between them and massaged her clit firmly, rhythmically, as he lifted his hips and pressed subtly upwards. Her hips picked up the rhythm of his stroking fingers, sliding her further and further onto his cock.

"I can't take any more," she moaned when she had less than half the length inside her.

"Sweetheart, you did good but you can do a little better. Another tiny piece and I will be satisfied." He kissed her as he held her hips and thrust upwards a couple of times. He felt her trying to raise herself away from the snake but he kept up his small thrusts until she pulled her lips away and gasped. He lifted her bodily onto his desk, still wedged inside her. Tweaking her nipples firmly as he kissed her deeply , he pressed slightly forward again—the further he got today, the easier the next time would be. He buried another inch inside her before she noticed the discomfort and moaned softly. He leaned down and kissed her as he slowly pulled himself out of her. "Don't be frightened, sweets— we'll save the rest for another day."

He straightened and pushed the snake back inside his black boxers.

"Now, I am going to make you cum harder than you did in the car." He pushed her pleated skirt up to get a glimpse of her sweet, deflowered young pussy. He was thankful that the black condom was concealing as well as slimming. He was sure she didn't realize she was bleeding. It was best not to alarm her unduly.

He wasn't into blood-sports but there was no other choice. He had to make her cum before she left. Finger-fucking was out of the question—she'd be too sore.

Think of it as a cut finger—suck on it to stop the bleeding.

He reached up and cupped her breasts as he covered her clit with his mouth.

***

Half an hour later, she sat quietly next to him in the car. The alcohol had almost worn off and she was beginning to feel the snake bite. He hadn't let her leave his office until she had cum twice so she had that pleasure to offset the bite.

"You okay?"

"I'm fine." Her voice was so soft he could barely hear it.

"Cassie, I hope you are not regretting what we did today." He undid her seatbelt and pulled her into his arms. "Honey, if Paul made love to you now, he wouldn't even know that you had a small piece of another man's penis inside you today."

"Really?" Her face brightened so considerably he felt no guilt at telling the outrageous lie.

"Trust me." He gave her a long, deep kiss. "Of course, I am hoping that you save yourself for me but I am grateful for what we had today. I'll understand if you don't meet me on Sunday."

"I will be there."

After those two mind-blowing orgasms, you bet your sweet fanny you'll be there!

"Honey, I'll wait an hour for you, if you don't turn up I won't think badly of you." He started the engine and pulled out of the parking lot.

"I'll be there even if I can't come to your house with you."

He reached across and squeezed her hand. "You are such a sweet girl, you deserve the very best and that's what I want to give to you."

He drove quickly, needing to head to LaBelle's as soon as he dropped Cassandra off. His two weeks with Marcia had officially expired the previous evening. He hadn't called to book her for an extra night, expecting that his snake would have been knocking at Cassandra's womb before the end of the evening.

Shit! Belle had indicated that there was already a list of men waiting for a taste of Marcia, two of them had even been willing to pay more than Graham had in an effort to get their hands on her a bit sooner but Belle had refused. Graham knew he'd be lucky if he got his snake into her tonight.

***

On Sunday morning he parked outside the public library and waited for Cassandra. God help her if she came back to his place today! Marcia had been too busy to fit him in on Friday evening. Belle had allowed him into her viewing parlour to witness Marcia's first double penetration. The two men, business partners, who had tried to outbid Graham in an attempt to get to Marcia sooner, had wasted no time in booking her for their favourite treat. Neither was particularly well endowed and after having Graham's much larger cock in both holes, Marcia had had little difficulty in climbing onto the younger partner's erection and leaning forward for the older one to push his modest tool into her posterior.

Graham had watched the action for a while but had been forced to go home and pet the snake himself. Usually he didn't mind masturbating but not after he had missed out on pussy. Belle had offered him another of her more experienced girls but he had politely declined. The girl she'd offered had been a favourite of his when she had first arrived at LaBelle's five years ago but she was now approaching 'retirement' age. He hadn't touched a woman over the age of twenty-one since his first time, when he had used an old hooker so that he'd know exactly what to do when his girlfriend finally agreed to let him stick his dick inside her instead of his finger.

When his girlfriend had consented, it had taken over an hour to accomplish the deed properly but that day, buried inside her tight, newly-opened pussy, he had known instinctively that he could never again stick his dick into another older woman. By the age of eighteen there was nothing he loved more than the feel of a tight pussy. Many of his male classmates had thought it uncool to be brainy and didn't consider him a threat even though he was blessed with incredible good looks. His looks and brains were a lethal combination, the girls at school couldn't resist him—only a handful escaped without at least a fingering. He deflowered a few of the more willing ones and thereafter screwed them as and when the opportunity presented itself. It got to the point where it became almost a juggling act to keep his girlfriend and his 'bits on the side' happy. It was a small wonder that he'd managed to keep his grades up, fucking a different girl almost every night of the week.

At university he specifically targeted the less-popular young women—especially the ones who had left the nest for the first time and were spreading their wings—he taught them how to fly.

One of the sweetest fucks he'd ever had was an overweight freshman, Nadine. Four months before he completed his doctorate he'd noticed her in the canteen with a few of her classmates. She was beautiful but just over two hundred pounds and the least trendy of the group. He had smiled at her kindly when their eyes met and she'd blushed. Immediately he'd gotten up and joined their table. Later that week he'd invited her to a burger bar and she'd accepted readily. He could tell that her friends were astonished by the attention he gave her, one of them had even tried hitting on him but he'd had no interest in the slimmer young woman who obviously already had several cocks under her belt.

Nadine had willingly come up to his small flat the first time he'd invited her. She had been a bit shy about taking her clothes off and he'd had to coax her to part with each garment, even while she was hidden under his duvet. When he had pulled the covers back and revealed her naked, voluptuous body he had almost cum instantly. She'd had round, firm breasts, a tiny waist and big hips and thighs. When he'd told her how incredibly sexy she was, she had rolled over to hide her blushing face in the pillows and exposed her perfect, pouting ass.

Like a dog in heat, Graham had pulled her upwards, buried his face between the big cheeks and eaten her pussy with vigour. She had literally screamed every time he'd flicked his tongue over her clit and when he slid a finger inside her she came after only two deep thrusts. He had plunged his cock inside her while she was still cumming, so quickly he was buried inside her before she had time to worry about the pain of losing her virginity.

Later, cuddled up to him, she'd confessed that she'd been the 'secret' mascot of her high school's basketball team for almost three months. The captain had pretended to be attracted to her and she had given him a blowjob after tutoring him in Maths one evening at her house. The next day he'd told all his team-mates about it. She had lived alone with her divorced mother who was a nurse and often did night shifts. It wasn't long before other members of the team were stopping by for blowjobs too. At first she had tried to refuse but they had let her know if she didn't comply they would spread the rumour around the school that she 'went down'. Already nearly a hundred pounds heavier than the average girl at the school she hadn't needed anything else to make her stand out even more, so she had indulged them, but had always remained fully dressed while the ballplayers just freed their cocks for her to suck on. Only one of them ever half-heartedly tried to finger her pussy. She had refused to let him and he had quickly lost interest. The fellatio-fest had ended when her mother had switched to working the day shift after being tipped off by a nosy neighbour who had seen the steady stream of buff, young men visiting the house at night.

Later, Nadine had knelt on the tiles in Graham's small shower and given him a blowjob that had almost blown his head off! He had barely managed to stagger weakly back to his bed, the blood pounding through his veins. She had followed on his heels like a bloodhound and promptly given him another.

He had been quite sad to say goodbye to his sweet Nadine. She had been the least demanding of all the young women he'd ever fucked. She used to come to his tiny cramped flat, cook him dinner and do her studies while he got on with his. If he still had his head buried in a book when she was ready for bed, she would have a shower and crawl into his bed, naked. Later, regardless of the hour, he would join her. Sometimes she would remain fast asleep as he fingered her but as soon as he pushed his cock inside her, she would awaken eagerly and have three or four orgasms before he finally thrust himself to a shuddering release.

She'd had one of the sweetest, tightest little assholes he had ever come across. She hadn't complained the first time he had slipped his finger into her ass while he was eating her pussy. So he had quickly slipped another one inside and continued. She had turned over and assumed the position when he had sat back on his heels to put on a condom. He had fucked her pussy quickly, using the deep, hard strokes that he knew made her cum fast but had saved himself for the ass-fucking to follow. He'd pulled his cock out of her pussy as soon as she came and she hadn't even murmured when he had put it against her asshole. Getting it inside her hadn't been an easy task. And each time after that seemed to give nearly as much trouble as the first—but he wasn't a man afraid of a little trouble, or a tight asshole.

He hadn't even realized that Nadine was losing weight until one of his colleagues made a sly comment one day about 'giving the poor girl a rest, or at least time to eat something in between fucking her'. That evening when she'd walked in, dressed in a figure-hugging denim dress, he had realized in shock just how much weight she had lost. He'd asked her if she was dieting and she said that it was the first time since the age of sixteen that she was not dieting but the weight had finally started to drop off. Of course, she'd added shyly, the regular workouts he was giving her were also helping to burn calories.

Even before he had left the university other guys had started sniffing around her. She had spent the summer holidays helping him furnish the house he had purchased and had burned off yet another dress size by the time she'd started her second year. He hadn't been surprised when she called him a week later and told him that their long-distance relationship wasn't going to work—she had been his only girlfriend for six months and he had given her a regular dose of cock—like a junkie, she needed a daily fix.

***

Ten minutes before the appointed time Graham saw Cassandra heading towards him, looking confident, her hips swinging. He never understood how parents didn't know when their daughters started screwing—it was always so obvious to him when the sweet, young virginal things he'd been eying had their first taste of cock. Cassandra had had only half a cock and already her walk had completely changed.

I'm getting pussy today!

Something in her walk told him that she was ready for the whole snake. She smiled as she recognized his car and hurried towards it. She slipped inside, quickly closed the door and turned eagerly as he leaned over to kiss her.

"I missed you so much, honey," he groaned against her neck. "Are you coming to my place or have you changed your mind?"

"I haven't changed my mind," she assured him.

"Good girl!" He straightened and fumbled with the key in the ignition. "I'm going to cook you lunch, something quick so that we can have time for ourselves. Do you like seafood?"

"I *love* seafood!"

"Great! I've bought a couple of lobsters and some tiger prawn."

"Lobsters! I love prawns but lobster is my favourite! I haven't eaten it in ages! My mother always complains that it's too expensive."

Your sweet pussy is worth the expense.

"I love it too, sweetheart. I was praying that you didn't have a shellfish allergy. I bought some chicken, just in case."

"I have no food allergies…at least none that I know of."

"Neither do I. See, we are meant to be together."

Okay, don't lay it on too thick. You are offering her some cock, not marriage!

He put his hand on her knee and stroked it before sliding his fingers under the hem of her dress. This time he didn't have to tell her to spread her legs. Slipping his fingers inside her panties, he massaged her clit, denying himself the pleasure of pushing a finger or two inside her. He didn't want to risk making her sore too soon—she'd be sore enough within the hour. He carefully teased her entrance with a fingertip and smiled as he felt her tilt her hips and try to press against it.

"Be patient, sweetheart. I know you can't wait to have my fingers inside you. When we get to my house I promise to *fill* your tight pussy with fingers," he vowed, subtly hinting that later when he forced several fingers inside her he would be doing so to please *her* not himself.

She blushed and he continued stroking her clit.

Ten minutes later he removed his hand to turn the car into his driveway. He took her up through the garage entrance as he had done Marcia, immediately turning to ask, "Would you like a glass of liqueur?"

"Yes, please." She licked her lips in anticipation. "It's so delicious."

"Not as delicious as you." He winked at her as he poured her a tall glass.

Handing her the drink, he left her to sip it as he prepared the ingredients. She sat on one of his kitchen high stools and watched him deftly put the meal together.

"Are you fully recovered from our little date on Friday?" he queried as he sliced a plum tomato.

"Yes."

"Good because I'd like you to take a bigger piece today." He closed the lid of the slow cooker and set the timer. "That will need about an hour. Once it's done I'll quickly cook the lobster and prawns. In the meantime let's have a bit of fun."

He picked up her drink and led her into his bedroom.

"Let me take off your dress, baby. I don't want to send you home rumpled." He turned her around and pulled the zipper at the back of her dress all the way down. He unhooked her bra, spun her around again and pulled the dress off her shoulders, the bra with it. She instinctively moved to cover her breasts but he took her hands in his and held them out of the way. "You have a beautiful body. I want to admire it all day."

If she was naked he would be able to plug her pussy every time she turned around.

"What about you?" she asked him.

"I was just about to take my clothes off."

He stripped down to his boxers and pulled her onto the

bed with him. Rolling on top of her, he kissed her passionately, raising his head to look into her eyes as his fingers found her nipples and tweaked them firmly. Still holding her gaze, he pressed his cock against her clit and rubbed suggestively. She answered by rubbing her clit back against his hard length.

"Did you enjoy my mouth on your pussy?" he asked, as if he needed to.

"Yes!"

"I'm glad because I can't wait to taste your sweet pussy again. I want to have some before and after lunch." He lowered his head to her nipples, tongued them briefly and raised his head. "I can't wait. Do you mind if I tongue your pussy now?"

"No," she answered shyly and glanced away as he pulled her to the edge of the bed and knelt between her legs.

Peeling her panties off, he spread her thighs a little wider than was necessary. Then he rained kisses up both inner thighs before settling his lips smack bang on her stiff clitoris, burying his face into her fragrant flesh. He stole a glance upwards. She had her eyes closed, not comfortable yet with having him put his mouth on her. The last time he had allowed her to keep her eyes shut—this time there was no blood to hide from her. When she was fully 'broken' he would let her be as shy as she wanted to be—it would enhance his pleasure but right now he wanted to turn her 'out'. "Put some pillows under your head and keep your eyes open for me. I want you to watch while I eat your pussy and give you the finger-fucking you begged me for in the car."

She cracked her eyes open and reached backwards to grab a couple of the big, fluffy pillows he liked to sleep on. He waited until she had positioned them comfortably under her head and was looking straight at him before he lowered his head and sucked on her clit like he was sucking on a juicy sweet. She gasped and moaned as he tongued her clit expertly. When her pussy was dripping wet, he held her gaze and carefully worked three fingers inside her. Her mouth opened soundlessly as he pressed them deeper. "I'm just keeping my promise, sweetheart."

No point in sparing the pussy because it was tight.

He went back to the skilful tonguing of her clit as he continued to finger-fuck her deeply, occasionally glancing up to ensure that she was watching. He needn't have bothered; she seemed enthralled by the sight. Just before she came he moved back onto the bed to wrap her in his arms and kiss her. He dipped his head, took a nipple into his mouth and sucked on it. Her hand shyly stroked him through his boxers. He covered it with his and pressed it more firmly against his rigid cock.

"Let me get a condom."

She sat up and watched him as he rolled it on, lying back and opening her legs as he turned towards her.

"I want you to be very brave for me—just like you were the last time. Remember, once we get past the pain there will be lots of pleasure." He kissed her as he held his cock and rubbed the head teasingly against her entrance. He intended to give her the whole thing but it didn't hurt to let her think that she had a say in the matter. "I want *you* to fuck me—work yourself onto my cock—you'll know when you've had enough."

He continued to stimulate the erogenous zones at her entrance as she moved wantonly against his cock-head. The slick feel of her pussy was driving him wild but he gritted his teeth and waited for her to press herself onto him. As soon as she did, he thrust forward and buried the head of his cock inside her.

"Yes, Cassie sweetheart, fuck me," he groaned as he leaned forward and sucked on one of her nipples again.

Rolling the other firmly between his fingers, he pressed slowly, slyly, deeper inside her as she pressed herself onto him.

Past the half-way mark and not a peep out of her. Except soft, throaty moans of pleasure.

Just over two inches to go and still no complains. But *fuck* her pussy was tight! Shit! He was going to shoot his load before…

Fuck! He collapsed onto her as his cock jerked and spilled his cum into the condom.

"Baby, you did well, you took a nice big piece." He kissed her as he eased out of her. "I think you can take it *all* the next time."

Her half-empty glass was making a neat watermark on his bedside table. He got off the bed, picked it up and handed it to her before going to dispose of the condom. He took a squirt of his favourite desensitizing spray before he made a quick sojourn to the kitchen to see how the meal was shaping up. Still twenty-five minutes left on the timer.

She was draining the glass as he walked into the bedroom. Good!

"Lunch is not quite ready," he informed her, going straight back to sucking on her nipples.

Immediately she reached out to stroke his cock. Such an excellent student!

"Now, let's try it the other way. I let you fuck me—now *I'm* going to fuck you."

He gloved up, positioned himself between her legs and slid inside her. As before, he got all but a couple of inches inside and then her tight pussy put up a fight. Impatiently he forced the remainder inside her to the hilt.

"Ow!" She looked up at him accusingly and pushed against his shoulders.

"Shhh! Lie still for a moment, baby, it will get better," he promised as he covered her lips with his, plunging his tongue deep into her mouth. He tweaked both nipples firmly as he kissed her, keeping his cock embedded inside her, waiting for her body to ease its tight grip. A few minutes later as he moulded her clit firmly between thumb and forefinger, he asked again, "Better?"

"Yes," she sighed, moving her hips in time with his fingers on her clit.

"I'm very proud of you," he complimented as he drew back slowly. He quickly sheathed himself fully and she gave a little scream, *as* he'd expected. He smiled secretly as he gave her another two wicked thrusts in quick succession. She gasped and clung to him tightly. Knowing that she was too caught up in the sensations he was creating within her body to think rationally, he tried to keep the laughter out of his voice as he said, "You aren't the only one feeling pain, Cassie, baby. Your pussy's gripping me so tight it hurts but if I pull it out now, the next time will be just as painful for both of us. I have to leave my cock inside you for a little while longer so that you will stretch properly. I have to bear the pain but let me do something to ease yours."

He moved his hand off her clit and reached under her to circle her asshole with a slick finger. Fucking Marcia had awakened his appetite for tight assholes. The thought of Cassandra's extra virgin anus innocently waiting to be discovered almost sent him insane! She had let Paul finger her pussy but Graham would bet a full month's salary that the young man had no idea of the pleasure to be found between Cassandra's firm, young cheeks. He intended to fully acclimatize her pussy to his cock before she left today and make a start on her ass with at least one finger, and another each time they met. If things went to plan, he'd be fucking her sweet asshole too in a matter of weeks.

"What are you doing?" she asked in alarm and clenched

her butt muscles.

"Trust me, honey, this will ease the pain and give you even more pleasure," he gently bit on a nipple as he pressed his finger harder against her. Her asshole was really extra virgin—he could barely get his fingertip inside it.

"Wrap your legs around my hips," he instructed and she immediately lifted her long, slim legs and curled them around his butt.

The new position opened the cheeks of her ass. Exerting gentle but firm pressure Graham breached the rim and slid the finger inside her. He thrust it back and forth for a while, feeling her pussy relax and her hips start to rotate again.

"Better?" he asked again.

"Yes," she breathed.

"Good. Now, lie back, relax and let me fuck you, honey. Let me show you what a special student you are. Your friends would be insanely jealous if they knew you were lying here with my cock buried inside you. They all want me to fuck them but I chose you because you were *so* sweet and innocent. You needed someone like me to fully awaken your desires. Now you are just like any *normal* teenager but very few of them would have had an excellent teacher to introduce them to the delights a cock can give, like you've had. Paul would have just ripped your pussy and given you no pleasure at all." He kissed her softly as she smiled happily at his words. "I'm so grateful for the honour of opening up your sweet pussy, I'm going to make you come even harder than before."

He started to thrust inside her carefully, not giving her the full length of his cock but rotating his hips in circles to increase her pleasure. She came within minutes but he tirelessly kept the motion up, still gently thrusting his finger inside her ass and sucking on her nipple just hard enough to enhance the other sensations. She had endured the pain, now she would enjoy the pleasure.

Until he took the pain to another level.

She moaned his name as she came yet again ten minutes later—one of her nipples deep inside his mouth; her legs still wrapped around his hips; his finger deep in her tight asshole; his cock squeezed into her pussy; her hips rotating to the rhythm he set. He quickened his pace and finally shot his spunk into the condom, glad that he'd had the foresight to desensitize his cock. Surely he would have shot his load again, ages ago.

***

Later that night he smiled as he remembered the day's beautiful conclusion. He had given Cassandra another round of cock as he had fed her lobster and juicy tiger prawns. He'd sat on one of his dining chairs and insisted that she sat on his lap while he fed her with his fingers. Since they were both naked, the only place for his erect cock to go was *up* inside her. He had stroked her clit and kissed her as she had lowered herself gingerly onto him. He had selflessly fed her most of the lobster as she seemed to enjoy it even more than he did. While she chewed and swallowed each mouthful he had sucked on her nipples or raised her slightly to plunge back inside her, slowly but deeply.

Then he had taken her back to bed to eat her pussy for dessert as he had promised earlier in the day. When he had spread the folds, her pussy had looked so swollen he'd decided that she'd had enough for one day. He had eaten her gently, considerately, like he had done the day he had taken her virginity in his office.

Lying with his arms wrapped around her afterwards he had started making plans for the summer holidays—that's when she'd dropped her bombshell. She was spending it in Europe, and on her return she would literally go straight on to university. Of course, another round of cock had immediately followed her statement! He had to make full use of her pussy before some randy European got his hand on it.

He had carried her to his luxurious bathroom to wash the scent of sex off her body. Her pussy had smelled so new and innocent after he had thoroughly washed it, he couldn't resist the temptation to tongue her sweet clit again. No more than he could resist the compulsion to rim her tight asshole and then push one, then two fingers inside it while she was bent over his bathtub with his cobra snaking its way in and out of her pussy. Driven to the brink of insanity by the squeezing tightness of her rim on his embedded fingers, he had pulled the cobra out of her pussy at one stage and tried to see if her asshole would allow it entry. Sadly, it hadn't.

He had dropped her off outside the library just before closing time so that she could borrow a few books before going home to mummy and daddy. Kissing her goodbye, he'd said that he was already looking forward to Friday—the last time they would meet before she travelled to Europe. He was going to fuck her in his office again. His desk was the perfect height for what he had in mind. First he'd lay her on it while he sat in his chair eating and finger-fucking her pussy until she came at least once, then he'd let her ride him until he came. He would rim her asshole while he got his wind back. Then he would take her from behind, finger-fucking her tight asshole at the same time, increasing the number of fingers in her ass as he continued to fuck her tight pussy. As soon as he managed to get a third finger inside her comfortably his cobra would strike! Once the head was in the rest would follow—he would see to it.

He couldn't wait for the sensation of her tight asshole painfully compressing his cock. He was mad at himself for waiting so long; he could have been fucking her regularly for at least a year. He had chosen to ignore the fact that she had a massive crush on him and would have been easily moulded into whatever he wanted. If he had followed his instincts and taken her to his place instead of home to her parents when he had offered her a ride home thirteen months ago, she would have been a fully-fledged freak by now. Quiet, shy girls were always more willing to please him once he 'broke' them right. Though only just-broken Cassandra already embraced his pleasure-pain principle: the greater the pain, the sweeter the resulting pleasure. In the coming weeks he would have tried her in every conceivable sexual position. Her young, flexible body would have been perfect for a few of the more uncomfortable, deeply penetrative positions he liked.

He couldn't wait to fuck her virgin ass.

Talking of asses, he should get down to Belle's for another round of Marcia's tight ass. The *nip* of Marcia's butt was heaven but Cassandra's pussy was just as *nippy*. It was the last time he would probably ever fuck Cassandra and desperately wanted the chance to break that virgin ass of hers but the longer he put off going to Belle's the more tricks Marcia would allow to have a go at that sweet little ass of hers now that he had shown her just how much more exciting a real throbbing cock was than a bottle neck.

He could hardly believe he was lying on his bed trying to decide which he would enjoy more: a young woman's almost virginal pussy or a young hooker's tight ass. They were both special to him—his cock had been the first ever inside either of them. Though he enjoyed a tight pussy, especially one that he had deflowered and had exclusive access to, there was something about a tight asshole that drove him crazy! What if Cassandra denied him the pleasure of breaking her ass on Friday? If she experienced any lingering discomfort from his attempt to push the cobra inside her ass today, she wouldn't be as keen on Friday. The problem with assholes is that unlike a sore pussy which could let out a stream of urine without much pain, a sore asshole lets you know that it's sore every time you shit. A former girlfriend had let him fuck her ass once, and then refused to even let him put as much as a finger inside it after that, not even after months of begging and pleading.

Marcia knew exactly what was required of her and seemed to crave it. She had needed none of the coaxing Graham usually wasted on young women just to get his cock inside their asses. She had been willing and eager.

It would be a pleasure to fuck the young hooker again. Graham smiled as he remembered the way her tight ass had kept trying to repel his cock. She was willing but her unruly ass was not—he would take great pleasure in fucking it until it learned obedience; fuck it regularly until it accepted the full length of his cock gracefully, with only a token resistance. Marcia's ass reminded him of sweet Nadine, whose asshole had put up a similar fight every time but finally he had tamed it a little by fucking it every day, sometimes twice if it put up too strong an opposition the first time or if she had her period. He would teach Marcia's unruly ass the same obedience.

He didn't mind Marcia using his cock as a guinea pig to perfect her deep-throat technique. And he certainly didn't mind fucking her ass regularly until he grew tired of it but he had to admit he preferred forbidden fruit. That's why Cassandra appealed to him so much. That's why most of his students appealed to him. His ultimate fantasy was Adele, an extremely gifted young student whom he would love to introduce to the delights of the flesh—his flesh in particular. She was the youngest student in the college, tantalizingly just under the age of consent but she looked at him with such admiration in her dark eyes—it would be easy to seduce her.

The trick would be to catch her just before she let someone else break...

Shit! Was this how it began?

You sleep with one student and get hooked. Then you start looking at younger and younger students?

But it was too late now...wasn't it?

Wasn't it?

***

Graham's sexual taste will never mature. He will always crave young, virginal flesh even as he grows old and wrinkled himself. All that stands between him and underaged children is the Law, but he will spend his life looking for vulnerable victims who are so barely legal it's a crime in itself. He has let his horniness overrule his common sense, now it's only a matter of time before he's caught with his trousers down, his cock in a minor.

This story originally contained gay sex but just before I published the book for the first time in April, 2007 I decided to amend it. I wasn't sure that straight men would want to read sex scenes which involved two men. More than a year later I was still not sure. So, I have given my readers, male and female—asexual, bi-sexual, homosexual or straight, a chance to read the original story by making it available in e-Book format.

*****

INTIMATE FRIENDS

I would have never doubted my sexual orientation if I hadn't fallen in love my first day at kindergarten. I remember clinging tearfully to my mother's hand, begging her not to leave me when a boy exactly the same height as I was came up and held my hand. He smiled at me and I let go of her and followed him meekly to the low table where he had been sitting playing with some building blocks.

"Honey, do you want me to stay for a while?" my mother had asked anxiously.

"I'm okay, Mom."

Understandably, she'd stared at me in shock after I'd delivered this seemingly simple statement—I had started crying the previous evening at the thought of being left alone at kindergarten with complete strangers and had only stopped in the car on our way over when she'd promised to stay with me until I was comfortable and to breast-feed me when we got home.

I was a late child, my brother was thirteen and my sister twelve when I was born. My parents had wanted a large family and had been trying for years after my sister's birth without success, so when my mother became pregnant with me, it was like a minor miracle. I was spoilt rotten from the day I first drew breath. I would scream loudly if I didn't get my way. I refused to stop breast-feeding even when I started on solids. Finally when I turned two my father insisted that I was too old to be sucking on my mother's breast but after a few sleepless nights he relented and let her give me one feed at night so that I could fall asleep. It might have gone on indefinitely if my parents hadn't gone out one evening and left my fifteen-year-old sister to baby-sit me. At bedtime she paced up and down my bedroom for hours with me screaming blue murder over her shoulder. Finally she had no choice but to let me suck on one of her breasts.

She was my father's little darling and I think she went crying to him as soon as my parents got home. The next evening my father put me to bed and sat patiently while I cried myself to sleep. I hated my sister for years—just because I'd sucked on her small, dry nipple for five minutes or so until I fell asleep, my father stopped my mother breast-feeding me. I should have bitten her!

The next day I went back to my old habit of putting my hand in my mother's bra and playing with one of her nipples while I sucked my thumb; something I had given up at sixteen months. This really worried my mother because she had read in some New Age book that children will stop breast-feeding when they were ready. She felt that I was traumatized in some way by the sudden cessation of being breast-fed, so during the day when we were home alone she would nurse me for a while. Even at that tender age I played her like a piano—if I fell over and hurt myself I needed to be breast-fed to stop crying. I would sometimes pretend to be sleepy just so she would cuddle me close and give me a nipple. Yet, I was somehow aware enough to realize that when my father or siblings were at home breast-feeding was not permitted. I hated weekends and holidays.

My mother picked me up at lunchtime after my first day

at kindergarten and all I talked about on the way home was my new friend Raymond. When we got indoors, she sat on her rocking chair, with me on her lap and pulled her breast out for my promised treat. *I* was as surprised as she was when I shook my head and said, "Don't want."

Just like that I abruptly stopped breast-feeding. It was as if I knew instinctively that Raymond had already stopped breast-feeding, therefore I should too.

My mother went back to work full-time the next month, much to my father's relief. At the time he'd worked as a manager at the Inland Revenue, he'd earned decent money but my mother was a chartered accountant and earned almost three times as much as he did. He had struggled to pay all the household bills when my mother had decided to take a career break when I was born.

Our parents believed in giving us the best in life: my brother had piano and judo lessons; my sister danced ballet and played the violin and I started French and piano lessons at the age of four. We lived in a four-bedroom house in Chelsea, one of London's more exclusive post codes and though both my parents worked in the City and travelled to work by public transportation, we always had two cars.

Raymond was the youngest of nine children. His poor mother always seemed to be doing some household chore or other. When I begged my mother to ask for him to sleep over I think his mother was so pleased to have one child less to look after, she readily agreed.

He and I spent the afternoon in my bedroom, playing with my toys and reading my books. Later, my mother put us both in the bathtub and bathed us together before tucking us in and reading us a bedtime story. I fell asleep with my arm around his sturdy little body, as happy as I could remember being. I had never shared my bed before, although sometimes I sneaked into my parents' bed. My father always brought me back to my own room at dawn because he liked to have a 'bit' in the morning, and once when I was younger he had been getting down to business and turned his head to find my eyes open watching him. My mother had told him that I was too young to understand what they were doing but my father insisted there had been a look in my eyes that made him think otherwise.

Raymond became a regular visitor to my house though I seldom went to his—my mother said she was scared that I would be injured in the rough-and-tumble of six older, rowdy boys. Secretly I think she worried that Raymond's mother would forget that I was visiting and somehow lose me. His two sisters were almost as tough as his brothers. Catherine, who was two years older than us always wrestled me into dark corners and kissed me, a fact she vehemently denied when we got older.

***

Raymond's parents were Catholic and I knew when he did his 11^+ exams they would want him to go to the top Catholic school in the area. I made my mother attend church services at their church for over a year so that I could be eligible to go to the same school, too.

Thankfully we both passed the entrance exam and the first week in September found us sporting matching outfits. Raymond was a natural athlete and quickly became one of the most popular boys at school, always picked first by any team captain. I hated it when we ended up on opposing teams. Cricket became our favourite game, I was a surprisingly good bowler; he was an excellent all-rounder. I panicked when I had to bowl the ball to him, worried that I would accidentally injure him. But by the second year he was regularly chosen to be captain and he always chose me first. A few of the boys made snide comments but by then my bowling had become so deadly no one questioned his decision. A few opposing captains decided to choose me first when given the chance—big mistake! In the end they called us 'The Dynamic Duo' and stopped trying to separate us. We lived up to our name in grand style; I would bowl a ball to an unsuspecting classmate who would lop it away thinking that it had slipped out of my hand—only to find that Raymond's, the safest pair of hands in the school, were cupped waiting for it to land in them. We were the youngest members of the school's cricket team. Our Physical Education teacher, Mr Bellows, started talking about us possibly playing for England when we were older and we basked in the glory.

It all came to a sudden end when a fifth former injured his spine in gymnastics, sued the school and won compensation. Although there were rumours that the boy did the complicated vault as a dare, none of his classmates who had witnessed the incident wanted to testify against him. The school immediately stopped all sports they considered potentially dangerous, including cricket. We were offered the option of playing soft ball—like we were girls! Of course, we turned it down!

My potential as a fast bowler crawled back and hid itself somewhere in my body. It never showed its face again. Raymond tried track and field events but this time he was alone in his sporting endeavours, I was content to cheer him on from the sidelines. He was a good sprinter but there were two other boys of the same age group who were better. They both beat him convincingly in the 100 and 200m races. He hated losing—two bronze medals ended his Olympic dreams.

***

When we were sixteen, I saw Raymond with a girl for the first time and my heart almost stopped. Up until then I hadn't given my feelings for him any thought. He was my best friend, I liked him more than I had ever liked anyone else, except my mother, and somehow we never seem to fight.

The girl, Tabitha, was from the nearby girls' school. She was a year older than us but Raymond was already six foot and very handsome. She held his hand and dragged him to a quiet street a corner away from the school compound. I followed them and watched her kiss him like she wanted to eat his lips.

The next day she sneaked us into her parents' house. She hadn't wanted me to tag along but Raymond had refused to go without me. They started petting on the sofa right next to me while I pretended to watch TV. They mostly kissed and fumbled in each other's clothing, nothing too shocking.

But within weeks she was doing everything but let Raymond enter her.

The first time she pulled his cock out of his trousers to stroke it I was so mesmerized by the sight of his erection I didn't even pretend to watch the screen. His cock was better looking than mine—straight while mine curved slightly.

I wish that was me. The thought flashed through my head as she daintily wrapped her lips around the head of his erect cock. But I wasn't wishing that she was going down on me—I was wishing that *I* was going down on him! Just like that, in a blinding moment, my first doubts about my sexual orientation took root.

Minutes later when Raymond was between her legs licking her pussy she turned to me and said, "Come here, shy boy."

At first I didn't move but Raymond raised his head and gestured me over. She pulled my head down to her bared breasts and I was forced to open my mouth and take her nipple into my mouth. I sucked on it hesitantly, remembering my last encounter with a small, non-lactating breast. I was very surprised when my cock got even stiffer. It must have been noticeable because Tabitha reached into my trousers and pulled it out.

"Look, Raymond, shy boy has a big cock!"

Raymond looked up from licking her pussy, glanced at my erect cock and then up at me. I couldn't be sure since his mouth was covered but I think he smiled. My first blowjob was over before it started. The feel of her mouth was completely different to the touch of my hand when I masturbated. I lasted a minute, tops. Tabitha barely managed to pull her head back before I shot my load. Thanks to the resilience of youth I was up again in a flash and she wasted no time trying to get me down again.

The two of us shared Tabitha for almost a year and a half, until she went away to university. I never 'went down' on her, there was an unspoken rule that Raymond, as her real boyfriend, should be the only one to have access to her pussy. But in all that time Raymond never stuck more than a finger inside her.

***

Pauline, Raymond's next girlfriend wasn't as accommodating where I was concerned. She complained that he spent too much time with me and wanted to know why I didn't have a girlfriend. So, I started dating Angel, a friend I had met years ago when we'd shared the same piano teacher. She was two years younger than I was and a real angel. When we went to the cinema, she and I just hugged and kissed while Raymond and Pauline made good use of the darkness.

As soon as I passed my driving test my mother bought me a brand new Volkswagen Golf GTi, much to my father's annoyance. That weekend we took the girls for a meal and then parked on a quiet residential street. Raymond and Pauline immediately started having sex on the back seat.

Angel and I necked in the front. For a slender girl she had amazingly big, round breasts like grapefruit halves. She must have been turned on by the sound of the two of them having noisy sex in the backseat because when I slipped my hand from her neck into the soft top she was wearing she didn't stop me. I quickly found her nipples and aroused them until they hardened into tight jelly beans but freeing her breasts from the underwired cups of her bra proved a task beyond me. She reached behind for the clasp and unhooked it herself.

Her breasts spilled into my hands and I nearly came. For a moment I wondered if my feelings for Raymond were exacerbated because I had never slept with a girl. Tabitha's small breasts had reminded me too much of my sister's—the same one that had put an end to my nightly breast-feeds. I loved Angel's big breasts, they reminded me of... Maybe my father had been right to stop my mother breast-feeding me. A young man shouldn't remember his mother's breasts. All I can say in my defence is that I never think of my mother's breasts in any kind of sexual way but my preference for big breasts may have been influenced by the comfort hers had given me.

Yet, even as I eagerly bent my head to take one of Angel's erect nipples into my mouth, I found myself looking through the gap in the front seats at Raymond's cock as it disappeared and reappeared as Pauline rode him like he was a stallion. Her ass was beautiful, big and round—at that moment I wished it was bony and flat—it was blocking my view of his cock.

***

When Angel and I had first started dating her mother had warned me that she would have me charged with statutory rape if I slept with her daughter, but even when she reached the age of consent, I didn't want to. She surprised me by telling me that she wanted me to be her first. Sod's Law, you beg a girl for sex and she never gives it up; never ask and *she* begs you for it! From all accounts a girl's first time was very painful and I didn't want to be responsible for giving her a bad experience.

I decided to ask my older brother, Robert, for some advice. He had been dating his wife, Kenya, since they were seventeen and he'd always locked me out of his bedroom door when he'd sneaked her in while our parents were at work. I have never met a more macho guy than my brother. I should have known better than to ask him for advice. He proceeded to give me an account of his first time with Kenya that made my hair stand on end. He described how he had struggled to get his penis inside her although he had made her very wet beforehand. He said his penis had hurt and her vaginal walls had squeezed him like a vice. By the time he got to the amount of blood she had lost—enough to soak through the towel, he had placed under her in anticipation, to his fitted sheet—I felt sick. I couldn't do that to Angel! Then he said very smugly, "You might not have the same problem—I have a big cock, I doubt yours is half as big."

Dropping my trousers and comparing hadn't seem a good idea at the time.

The week before I left to start university Angel became a bit more persistent. I think she got it into her head that I would stay faithful to her during my years as a horny undergraduate if we slept together first.

Finally I asked Raymond for some advice. I knew Pauline hadn't been a virgin when they had started dating, I didn't think he'd had any firsthand experience but I was desperate. I couldn't believe it when he admitted that he'd taken Tabitha's virginity when she had come down for the Christmas holidays during her freshman year.

This information hurt me deeply and I still don't know

why. It wasn't as if I had been there the first time he had screwed Pauline and I wasn't there when they did most times, except for when they did it in the backseat of my car. I felt betrayed by the fact that he had seen Tabitha without me being there, although I suspected that she'd asked him to come over alone. It hurt that he had kept the secret for almost a year.

Thankfully, Angel started her period two days before I left for university so the topic of sex was dropped.

***

Raymond and I attended the same university but he did Computer Science while I did Telecommunications. We had both planned to do Engineering but he got a C in A-Level Maths and had to revert to his second choice of degree. I tried to change courses as well as soon as I realized that we wouldn't be together but the tutor told me the computer course was too full—later, I found out the bastard had lied to me. The Engineering department wasn't attracting the numbers the college required so they had refused to let me switch disciplines.

I could barely keep my concentration on my lectures. I kept thinking of Raymond, wondering who he was with and if he was missing me as much as I was missing him.

Although the university was near enough for me to travel from home each day, my mother had decided that it would be a good experience for me to live away from home. She had planned to rent a one-bedroom place but the letting agent found a small two-bedroom flat that cost just slightly more. I persuaded her to rent it so that Raymond and I could share. My father was a little concerned about my friendship with Raymond but my mother found it perfectly natural. She'd been worried about me being on my own for the first time, Raymond being so close at hand reassured her.

I loved sharing the flat with Raymond. Most days we

cooked dinner together in our small kitchen after lectures. He was a good cook; he and his siblings had shared household duties as soon as they were old enough. At first I couldn't boil an egg—we'd had a maid for most of my life, but I quickly learned my way around the house. I was the one who would do our laundry and then stand for hours on Sunday ironing while Raymond flicked from one sport channel to the other on the television. I would also be the one doing the dishes—though sometimes he would jump up onto the counter and chat to me while I was washing up.

He had girls over regularly and because the flat was so small it was impossible not to hear what they were getting up to. I used to lie in my bed and masturbate listening to the sounds coming from his room. I would never picture the women naked; my thoughts were always filled with Raymond's fit bitter-chocolate body. I would imagine him over me, leaning down to kiss me, his cock rubbing deliciously against mine. I wasn't naïve but I never at the time gave anal sex a thought, what I wanted most was for him to kiss me, for us to lie naked in bed together, wrapped in each other's arms. I wanted us to engage in mutual masturbation and maybe give each other blowjobs.

***

There was only one openly gay young man on my course and I avoided him like the plague. He was too loud, too effeminate. Yet, somehow he always managed to sit next to me or get partnered with me whenever we had to work in pairs in the lab.

One day he asked me outright if I was in love with Raymond. I was so shocked I couldn't lie fast enough. He gave me a knowing look and told me that it was perfectly understandable—Raymond was divine!

His name was Edwin but he told me that the older, married man who was fucking him liked to call him Edwina.

He had met the man in, I think he said Epping Forest, I wasn't paying much attention to that detail at the time—my mind was still trying to come to grips with the fact that a married man would sleep with another man.

"Why doesn't he leave his wife if he's gay?" I asked Edwin.

He rolled his eyes and asked me what planet I had dropped to earth from, then explained that the man was bi-sexual.

That night I started thinking that maybe I was bi-sexual and not gay as I had previously thought. I loved Raymond but I also loved Angel. She was the sweetest girl I had ever met. I loved kissing her and whenever she let me play with her breasts I was in seventh heaven—I never got tired of sucking on her nipples. It wasn't as if I hadn't wanted to make love to her, it was just that I didn't want to be the one 'plucking' the cherry. I have always been a little squeamish and the thought of all that blood had put me right off the idea. We were still dating but I'd had exams on my return to university after the Christmas holidays so I had spent the break studying. I spent a little more time with her during the Easter holidays and the subject of sex came up again. She accused me of not wanting to make a commitment to her.

I was almost hoping that she would sleep with someone else before I went home at the end of the first year—get the first time over and done with. But the thought of her with someone else filled me with jealousy. My father always told my mother than I never learned to share because she'd spoilt me rotten, he was right.

After lectures one day I was bursting for a leak, I rushed out of the classroom and headed for the nearest gents. I heard a strange, choking sound while I was peeing in one of the urinals and looked up to find Edwin staring at my cock. Up until this point I had made an effort to avoid going to the bathroom with him, not wanting my fellow students to think that we were getting up to anything while we were there.

He walked into one of the stalls as I shook the last drops of urine from my cock and pushed it back into my boxers.

"Psst!"

I looked around and he had the door of the cubicle open and was gesturing me over. I hesitated for a second. It was just the two of us in the bathroom and maybe, I reasoned, he needed some loo roll or something. *Or* so I tried to convince myself, later.

I walked over to him and he quickly pulled me into the stall and locked the door.

"Let me give you a blowjob," he whispered.

He sat on the closed lid of the loo, put his hand in my track bottoms and pulled my cock out. He didn't even wipe it or check to see if it smelled, he just put his mouth on it and started. While giving me head he took his own cock out and masturbated himself with one hand. It was scary to see the whole of my erect cock disappear into his mouth—he behaved as though he literally wanted to consume it!

I had fantasized about Raymond giving me a blowjob but I was unprepared for the reality of another man giving me head. I was battered by two extreme emotions: I felt disgusted, yet his expertise excited me. I was surprised when he swallowed; Tabitha never had.

I didn't realize that he had squirted on me until I saw him reach for some tissue and try to mop it up as I leaned weakly against the door of the stall. It was the first time I had cum while standing up and it felt as if he had sucked my energy out of my body along with my semen.

I looked at my watch and cursed. Raymond would have been waiting for me in the library for at least five minutes.

"I've got to go," I told Edwin and rushed out of the stall.

It only occurred to me as I made my way across campus

that I hadn't thanked him for the blowjob. And worse, not even checked to see if there was anyone else in the bathroom before I'd rushed out!

"Lecture run late?" Raymond queried as I hurried into the library breathlessly minutes later.

I opened my mouth to say yes, instead I heard myself say, "No, I was with Edwin."

What can I say? I have never been able to lie to him.

He looked at me curiously for a second and then said, "Be careful."

He grabbed his rucksack and headed for the exit. I couldn't tell what he was thinking. He didn't seem angry or surprised, or jealous, as I had vaguely hoped. We chatted as normal on the way home. I tried to bring the topic of Edwin up but somehow couldn't comfortably squeeze it into the conversation.

The previous day we had made spaghetti bolognaise. Raymond had said that half the packet of pasta would be enough, I had disagreed. He'd been right, so we had enough for two days. Twice I caught him looking at me while we ate, which was not unusual—but him looking away hastily when I looked back at him *was*.

***

Edwin kept pestering me to meet him in the gents again and it was hard to resist the temptation. Tabitha had sucked my dick; Edwin had given me head—huge difference! After seven weeks of holding out, I finally gave in.

Raymond had left for London just after his last lecture at one o'clock that day. I had been invited to his older sister's birthday party but I was trying to avoid going to London—I had promised Angel that we would sleep together the next time I came down.

This time when Edwin got my cock erect he stopped and asked me if I wanted to have anal sex with him. I shook my head automatically, thinking that he would get back to the blowjob but he started pleading with me.

"I don't have a condom," I protested, certain that he wouldn't either.

Wrong! He whipped one from the pocket of his jeans before I could finish the sentence. I was well and truly trapped. I could have walked if I wanted to—physically he was no match for me but part of me was a little curious. Why did I love Raymond so much? And why unlike most young men I wasn't biting at the bit at the thought of taking a girl's virginity?

It was awkward to manoeuvre in the small space but finally I had the condom on me and he was in front of me, bent slightly at the waist, his hands braced against the walls. He had wanted me to sit down on the loo and let him sit on me but I quickly vetoed that option. I stood for a minute looking down at his ass but couldn't bring myself to do it. I felt my erection deflating and was about to tell him to forget the whole thing when he reached backwards, positioned my cock against his asshole and pressed back against me. I was shocked at the speed with which I found myself buried in his heat. I stood there stupidly, doing absolutely nothing as he moved backwards and forwards. I felt like I was having an out-of-body experience. Even when I came minutes later, it felt remote and strange, like a dream.

I quickly pulled myself out of him. The stall suddenly seemed too small and I was anxious to get away from him. He turned around and leaned up, I think to kiss me but I pushed him away.

I had been about to walk away without a word, like I had done the first time but someone walked into the gents as I reached down to unlock the door. Edwin and I stood silently staring at each other while the guy peed, then farted loudly. When he left without washing his hands, we couldn't help the laughter that erupted from us as soon as the door closed behind him.

Deciding that I needed to talk to Edwin, I let him leave first and head to a nearby pub. I joined him in less than five minutes and we ordered a pint of lager each.

"We're not doing that again!" I blurted out as soon as we sat at an empty table. "I didn't enjoy it."

"You came, didn't you?" he mocked me.

"I had to pretend I was in a *pussy*!"

"*Raymond's* pussy?"

I almost decked him before I realized he was just teasing me.

"Maybe you are like me," he suggested.

I didn't have to ask what he meant, the very thought had occurred to me while making my way over to the pub. Was I one of those men who other men fucked and not the other way around? Girly Edwin had been the aggressor back there in the stall. I had simply stood meekly and let him take control.

"My friend would love to meet you."

"You told your friend about me?" I asked in alarm.

"No. I mean if you want to see…you know…I could ask him to meet you."

I must have been a little tipsy by the time we had ordered a third round because I suddenly found myself talking to his friend on his mobile phone and agreeing to meet him later.

"You will love Andre. He is a total whore but he has a big cock and he can *fuck*!"

Edwin was behaving 'gayer' with every sip of lager he took and there was a group of four men who had 'homophobia' written across their foreheads. One false move or look and they would kick the shit out of us. I decided it was time for us to leave. Plus, I wanted to go home as soon as possible so that I could get dressed to meet

Andre.

***

I changed my mind while standing under the shower.

I can't stand pain. My reluctance to make love to Angel was not purely altruistic, the thought of her pussy painfully squeezing my cock gave me as many sleepless nights as the thought of the blood she would shed.

I had been constipated once—the most unpleasant experience of my life. When I had finally passed the stool, I had looked down to see what had given me so much grief. It hadn't been that big—nowhere near the size of my cock and it had hurt like hell! I remembered Edwin's words...*he has a big cock...*

Did he mean bigger than mine? I hope not! I dialled Andre's number but it went straight to voicemail; he must be already on his way over.

He arrived half an hour late. He was good looking but arrogant. Of course, *not* as good looking as Raymond.

"Would you like a glass of wine or a beer," I asked as he took a seat in the armchair across from me.

"You ain't got nuthin fuh eat?" His voice shocked me. He was African, possibly from the Ivory Coast or other French-speaking country but had a fake Jamaican accent.

I hadn't realized that it was a proper date and that I'd be expected to cook! Luckily, I had some fried chicken in the fridge. I warmed four pieces and put them on a plate with some potato salad for him. He ate like he hadn't seen food in days and it unnerved me slightly. He quickly downed a bottle of beer and gave an appreciative manly belch.

"Get one thing straight, I ain't no fucking homo—I ain't kissing you or sucking your dick!" he informed me immediately after the manly belch.

I wasn't sure if I wanted to kiss him either so I didn't object to the first part of the statement but I had anticipated that he would have sucked my dick after I had sucked his. I had expected some sort of touching...

He touched me alright—pushing me to my knees as he pulled his cock out of his fly. It wasn't so much *big* as it was fat. All things considered I would have preferred length to girth.

I wrapped my hand around it and stroked it. It quickly hardened but I couldn't bring myself to put my mouth on it—the thought that it had been in another man's ass put me off. I told him I couldn't go down on him.

"Turn round and drop your pants then."

I stood up and stared at him.

"Aren't you going to use a condom?"

"Yuh got one?" he asked impatiently.

"Yes," I replied and quickly went into Raymond's room to raid his stock.

I grabbed two and returned to the living room, making sure that he put one on before I dropped my jeans and boxers and leaned over the chair. I thought he would prep me with a finger or two first. Instead, the 'Ruff Ryda' tried to prep me with his fat cock. He pressed hard against my asshole and pain ten times worse than constipation shot through my body like an electric shock.

I pushed him off and straightened immediately.

"What are you doing, bitch?" he asked angrily, dropping the fake accent.

"I-I've changed my mind," I stammered.

"Changed your mind? I am not leaving here with a hard cock—so you'd better start sucking."

"Look, I'll give you some money and we'll forget the whole thing," I suggested, wanting him out of my flat as quickly as possible.

"Give me the money then!"

I had seventy pounds in my pocket. I offered him fifty

but he grabbed the other twenty as well. I let him, thinking that he would leave. He pocketed the money and then started waving his dick around. "You are still going to suck my dick, bitch. Like I said—I'm not leaving here with a hard cock."

He could leave with no cock, period! The fool obviously hadn't seen *The Shawshank Redemption.* For that fact alone he deserved to lose his fucking dick. I pulled myself up to my full height—all 5'11½" of it, and had about three inches on him. "Just leave, okay."

He pushed his cock into his fly and I breathed a sigh of relief. His punch caught me square on the jaw. I never saw it coming. I staggered backwards, fell over the chair but landed unhurt on the carpet on the other side.

He moved around the chair but I was on my feet, waiting. He swung again. I grabbed his hand, twisted it behind his back and caught him in a neck hold. Silently I thanked my macho shithead of a brother for the years he had spent trying to turn me into a little macho shithead like him.

"You can leave with the money I gave you or you can leave without it, make up your fucking mind!" I warned as I marched him to the front door.

Thankfully he reached out to open it himself. I chucked him out and quickly locked the door. Immediately he started trying to kick the shit out of it. Counting to ten, my jaw beginning to throb like it was broken, the rim of my asshole burning like it was on fire, I tried to calm myself. Just as I was about to open the door and push him down the fucking steps—he stomped down them voluntarily.

I had never been angrier with myself!

Another shower calmed me down a bit. I crawled into bed to lick my wounds, wishing that I was a dog so that I could have licked my ass as well.

My mobile phone rang and I reached to answer it

automatically.

"What the hell were you playing at?" Edwin was so angry, I barely recognized his voice. "I tried to do you a fucking favour!"

"Your friend is a fucking piece of shit!" I was immediately furious again. "He is the worst fucking combination in the world—a *homophobic* homo. I feel sorry for the bastard!"

He immediately hung up on me. I didn't give a shit! How a gay man could have a friend like Andre was beyond me. I'd thought that I was confused: in love with Angel but wondering if I was gay; Andre was even more so—thinking that he was straight yet pushing his cock into other men's assholes. His scorn for gay men probably came from the deep-seated knowledge that he was one too. I should have done him a favour—overpowered him and fucked his ass for him.

***

I spent the weekend cleaning the flat, trying to rid it of the memory of Andre and my complete lack of judgement, wishing that Raymond was there. I wouldn't have been foolish enough to invite Andre over if Raymond had been home, but if I had done and Andre had squared up to me, Raymond would have kicked his ass like it was a football. He had always fought my battles for me, so it had come as a shock to me when I had instinctively fought Andre back, I'd never had to fight anyone before.

When Raymond came back late Sunday evening I was in my room watching TV. He pushed my door open and popped his head around it.

"You missed a great par—" he broke off and stared at me for a minute. "What happened to you?"

I should have realized that he would notice my swollen jaw.

"You don't want to know." I evaded giving him an answer.

He came into the room and stood looking at me for a minute as if he thought that I would elaborate. When I didn't, he said, "Angel was disappointed not to see you at the party."

"I didn't know she was going to be there."

"Catherine invited both of you," he reminded me.

"I know, but I didn't think she'd go on her own."

"She didn't."

"*What?*" I must have misheard him!

"She brought a guy with her."

"What *guy?*"

"She introduced him to me—I think his name was Simon. The music was loud, I couldn't hear her properly."

This information totally fucked up an already fucked-up weekend. My two forages into the gay world hadn't gone as expected and I was beginning to wonder if I was mistaken about my sexuality. Angel had been nagging me to let her come up for a weekend but I had found every excuse under the sun for her not to. In bed Friday night after Andre had left, I had decided to invite her up for the next Bank Holiday weekend.

"Don't tell me you're *jealous?*" Raymond asked in surprise. "You have been messing around with Edwin, I thought you didn't want Angel anymore."

The next thing I knew I was telling him the whole sad story. What can I say? I have never been able to lie to him.

***

Friday evening we spent a few hours in one of the local sports bars as usual but at half past eight Raymond got up and said, "Let's go."

"Where are we going?" I asked as I started my Freelander and pulled away from the kerb.

He gave me an address and I mentally tried to work out the quickest route to it.

"We're going to visit a hooker," he added casually.

"*What?*" I asked in alarm, just managing to avoid a parked car as I momentarily lost all sensation in my body and control of the vehicle.

"Her name is Geraldine and she sounds nice."

"You want *me* to screw her?" I asked, imagining him watch me as I made a complete fool of myself.

What if I don't get an erection?

"Don't worry, we'll screw her together."

That was more like it! My cock immediately hardened at the thought.

Forty-five minutes later we pulled up in front of her house.

She looked and sounded nothing like I'd expected a prostitute to. She was late thirties, quite good looking and surprisingly well spoken and cultured. She invited us in and led us straight to a bedroom on the ground floor. Raymond had obviously discussed terms with her in advance because he pulled some money out of his pocket and handed it to her without counting it.

"Condoms are on the nightstand," she informed us as she quickly counted the money.

"We brought our own." Raymond pulled an unopened box from the inner pocket of his jacket.

She took it and checked the expiry date. "OK, you can use those."

We stripped off and for the first time in years I saw Raymond's cock. It was a little bigger than the last time I'd seen it but it was still as gorgeous as ever. I had wondered if Andre had put me off the idea of giving Raymond head; one look at his chocolate stick and I knew that I definitely still wanted to taste it.

Raymond stood behind Geraldine and slipped her robe off her shoulders. I was disappointed to see that she had breasts the size of a young teenage girl but it didn't stop me from moving across the room and bending to take a nipple into my mouth.

I felt us moving backwards and realized that Raymond was steering us towards the bed. We climbed onto it and I went back to sucking on her nipple. Raymond reached for my hand and the next thing I knew I was touching a pussy for the first time. It was wetter than I had expected. He kept his hand on mine as I stroked what I presumed was her clitoris. When I timidly pushed a finger inside her following his tacit instruction, I found her soft and warm.

Geraldine sat up and reached over for the condoms. She rolled one onto me with her mouth and turned over to roll another onto Raymond. He caught my eye and imperceptibly signalled her raised hips. Her ass was sticking up in the air, her shaved pussy like a dark brown rose peeping out from between her legs. I didn't stop to think, I just got behind her and pressed my cock against her. She reached back, positioned the head properly and I slid inside her quicker than you could say, one, two, three.

I came almost as quickly.

She had been giving Raymond head during my brief fuck, and as soon as I pulled my cock out, he pulled her onto him. I watched her ride him, amazed that he didn't cum within minutes like I had done as she rotated her hips and moved up and down on him.

"Do you do double penetration?" I asked, shocking us all.

She stopped and stared back at me, the shock still on her face, probably thinking what a nice college boy like me knew about DP. "That will cost fifty pounds extra."

"No problem."

I grabbed my jeans and put the money on the nightstand.

"Go and take off the condom," she ordered, indicating the en suite bathroom.

When I came back she pulled herself off Raymond, opened the bottom drawer of the nightstand and took out a foil paper containing a sterile wipe. Ripping it, she wiped my rock-hard-again cock.

In case you are wondering what a nice college boy like me knew about DP—not a damn thing! But I had watched a documentary on Channel 5 and remembered a guy saying that he couldn't do it. The thought of another man's cock rubbing against his put him off the idea; the same thought turned me on to the idea.

She rolled one of her own condoms onto me with her hand. Raymond looked at her questioningly and she explained, "These are much stronger, they won't rip accidentally."

He had to withdraw almost fully for me to eventually get my cock into her ass. It was much tighter than her pussy had been, even with plenty of lubricant on the condom. The thicker condom didn't stop me from cumming quickly again but I left my cock inside her, enjoying the feel of Raymond's rubbing along its length. Of course, that made me hard again. Raymond's thrusts quickened as he was about to cum and I came again.

"I thought you said you didn't like anal sex," he commented, pulling the seatbelt over his broad chest as I pulled away from the kerb.

"I thought I didn't." Geraldine's smooth ass had felt much nicer than Edwin's but it was the delicious friction of Raymond's cock rubbing against mine rather than her hairless ass that had made the experience more enjoyable for me.

"I couldn't have anal sex," Raymond stated.

My hopes would have been dashed there and then if Andre hadn't completely put me off that particular notion. His nose flaring slightly as if he found the thought distasteful, Raymond asked, "What did it feel like?"

"Almost the same as her vagina except tighter."

Raymond nodded as he absorbed this information.

We drove in silence for the rest of the way but when he entered the flat he turned and asked, "Do you think you're gay?"

"I don't know," I answered honestly. I had never felt an attraction for any other male but whenever Raymond walked around the flat in his boxers I still found myself drinking in the sight of his naked chest and muscular legs.

***

We went back to Geraldine's the next Friday and had pretty much a repeat of the previous week, except that I went straight for her ass while Raymond enjoyed her pussy.

The following Friday as we walked to college I turned to Raymond and said, "I've booked Geraldine for nine o'clock but she's only free for half an hour."

"Tariq, we can't keep going to Geraldine's. I wanted to help you sort your sexuality out *not* get you hooked."

"OK," I agreed, "We'll go tonight for the last time."

Geraldine opened the door as soon as Raymond pressed the bell. Knowing that we were running against the clock, we took our clothes off immediately.

"Don't you guys have girlfriends?" she asked as we made a sandwich with her as the filling, our erect cocks poking into her.

"I have a girlfriend," Raymond replied, palming her breasts in his large hands.

I didn't answer. I hadn't spoken to Angel since Catherine's party three weeks ago. I missed her but I was pissed off at the thought that she might have let Simon fuck her.

"Guys, let's try something different, it's my birthday and I don't want to go to bed with a sore ass tonight."

Geraldine's words took a moment to sink in.

No fucking way! Disappointment almost deflated my cock but her next words made it harden to the point of pain. She took both of our cocks in her hands and said, "It would give me the greatest pleasure to see you guys play with each other's cocks."

Geraldine offered Raymond's stiff cock to me. I looked at him to see his reaction but she didn't give me time to gauge his thoughts. She grabbed my hand and wrapped it around his cock, moving it backwards and forwards. His cock felt like silk-wrapped steel, when she took her hand away I continued without missing a beat.

"Come on, Raymond, you do the same for your friend."

To my surprise he grabbed my cock and started stroking it in pretty much the same way I was stroking his.

It felt *so* good!

"Look at you guys, best buddies jerking each other off and loving it."

We stopped immediately at the sound of her voice—I could have slapped her!

"OK. Now I'm going to give each of you the best blowjob you've ever had," she said pushing us towards the bed.

She wrapped her right hand around my cock and urged me a little closer as she took Raymond's cock into her mouth. Less than a minute later she pulled it out slowly, ran her tongue around the head and offered it to me. This time I didn't check for Raymond's reaction, I pulled it deep into my mouth and cupped his balls.

I'd expected an epiphany: a feeling of homecoming, a sense of rightness when I finally wrapped my lips around his cock but I was disappointed—it felt like I was sucking on a big, warm but tasteless lollipop that filled my mouth, threatening to choke me.

Geraldine quickly moved down the bed and took my cock into her mouth. Raymond ran his hand up her leg and pushed his fingers inside her pussy. I looked up and caught his eye as he watched me give him head. He seemed in shock but I had wanted to do this for so long it would have taken several punches around the head to get me off him.

Geraldine knew how to give head—I tried to hold out but her mouth on my cock and mine on Raymond's was... I shot my load just as Raymond grabbed my head with his free hand. I think he'd meant to push me away but somehow ended up holding my head in place for the first spurt of his cum. I pulled back instinctively as it hit my throat and the second caught me *almost* in the eye. Thinking of the mess it would make I quickly covered his cock again and caught the third spurt, swallowing automatically.

Finally his cock stopped jerking, I let go of it and got off the bed. Our gazes caught and I couldn't tear my gaze away from his shocked, slightly pitying eyes.

"Well, guys, your time is up."

This time I was grateful for the sound of Geraldine's voice, I used it as an excuse to look away. I paid her and we left without speaking.

We were both still silent as I started the vehicle and drove off. Raymond had his face turned towards the window, his whole body tense.

Suddenly he shouted, "Pull over!"

My heart leapt in my chest. I thought he wanted to throw up but as I quickly parked between a Ford Mondeo and a Nissan Micra, he turned to face me. He looked at me for a minute in silence—it felt like twenty to me—and then said finally, "Tariq, you are my best friend. If you are gay I don't have a problem with that, but I am not. Don't *ever* fucking do that again!"

"Don't worry, I won't." Weak with relief that he hadn't said our friendship was over I blurted out, "Your sperm tasted horrible!"

"*Good*!" he said spitefully.

We looked at each other in surprise and then we both started laughing. I started the vehicle but had to pause before pulling out as another burst of laughter shot through me.

Angel was waiting outside the flat when we got there, her head sleepily resting on her overnight case. I was surprised how my heart contracted at the sight of her.

"What time did you get here?" I asked lifting her up into my arms as Raymond took the travel case.

"About an hour ago."

"Why didn't you call my mobile?" I doubted that I would have heard it while I had my lips wrapped around Raymond's cock but I would have seen the missed call when I checked my phone afterwards.

"I forgot mine at home and couldn't remember your number by heart."

"Are you hungry?" Raymond asked as he headed towards the kitchen.

"No thanks, Ray. I just need a shower and to rest for a while."

I carried her to my bedroom and placed her on the bed.

"You don't seem very pleased to see me." I could tell that she was making an effort not to cry. I felt terrible but I didn't want to kiss her with the taste of Raymond's cum still in my mouth. "Shouldn't I have come?"

"I'm glad you're here," I tried to reassure her. "I'm just surprised that's all."

"Right." Her lower lip began to tremble. "Where's the

bathroom?"

"I'll show you."

She stripped down to her underwear, wrapped a towel around her body and grabbed her toiletries bag. I held her hand and led her to the small bathroom Raymond and I shared, locking the door when we got inside. She turned to me in surprise. "What are you doing?"

"Joining you, I need a shower too."

I grabbed my toothbrush, squeezed a generous blob of toothpaste on it and started brushing my teeth. As I stripped and jumped into the shower, Angel took her toothbrush out of its travel case. I quickly soaped my body, trying to get rid of any lingering smell of Geraldine's perfume. Then I turned and looked at Angel as though surprised she was still outside the cubicle. "Hurry up, I'm waiting!"

"You'll get my hair wet," she complained.

Her hair was braided into tiny plaits and pulled back into a ponytail.

"I'll be careful," I promised and finally, she smiled.

"Turn around," she ordered, suddenly shy.

Dutifully, I averted my eyes and within seconds she had squeezed in beside me.

"I'm really glad you came," I said and kissed her. "I missed you."

"You couldn't have missed me that much or you would have come to Catherine's party!"

"I had a few things to do." Like getting punched while exploring my sexuality. "I would have come if I could have."

"I thought maybe you didn't want to see me." I watched her run the soapy flannel across her breasts and my cock hardened.

"Is that why you took *Simon* to the party?" Damn, my voice sounded jealous even to my own ears.

"My cousin *Simeon*—you've met him at my house

before!"

"Simeon?" Her lanky cousin who wore the thickest lens known to man!

"Mum insisted that I took him with me."

I smiled. Raymond always complained about girls' fathers giving him the third degree; Angel's father was fine, her mother was the Rottweiler. "I'm surprised she let you come up to visit me."

"She didn't want me to," Angel admitted, "but I reminded her that you've been my boyfriend for over three years."

Three years and I hadn't made love to her? Have I been doing drugs?

Suddenly keen to get her between the sheets, I took the flannel and finished soaping her body. Rinsing her quickly, I turned the water off and grabbed her fluffy pink towel off the rack. I handed it to her before using mine to hastily cover my embarrassingly stiffening cock. I hurried her along to my bedroom and was about to close the door when I remembered condoms.

"I'll be back in a second."

Raymond was in bed watching the news when I tapped on his door. He lowered the volume as I entered the room.

"I need some condoms."

"Go ahead." He gestured to the bedside unit. I quickly walked over and grabbed an opened box.

"Thanks."

Closing the door behind me, I started for my room when I heard him call my name.

"Don't make love to her if you are not sure," he warned, looking like he would beat me up if I messed with her.

He treated Angel like she was his little sister. I understood his concern, it had been part of the reason why I had hesitated to sleep with her—I hadn't wanted to take her virginity and then realize that I was gay after all.

"I'm sure."

***

She was waiting with the duvet pulled up to her neck. Quickly dimming the light, I dropped the towel and got in beside her. I turned to look at her and realized that I hadn't dimmed the light sufficiently. Her face looked as worried as I felt.

Then I remembered the blood. The towel I'd used was lying on the floor, close enough for me to reach, but it was damp. I got off the bed again, grabbed one from the bottom drawer of my wardrobe and jumped back into bed with it clutched in my hand.

I turned to face her again and she looked even more worried.

"We don't have to do it." Now that the moment had come I felt nervous.

"I want to, but I have something to tell you first," she whispered. She moved closer and laid her head against my chest.

"Go ahead," I encouraged, pushing her braids off her face to see her properly.

"I fell out of a tree when I was eleven...I was spending the summer holidays with my aunt in Bermuda...," she stopped and buried her face into my shoulder for a few minutes. I felt her shudder before she continued, "...when I woke up the next morning there was blood on my panty. I thought maybe my period had started but it hadn't."

I didn't understand what she was trying to tell me. "So...?"

"I hit the ground really hard—I think I lost my...my hymen."

"It doesn't matter." I was relieved, yet vaguely disappointed. I had finally worked up the courage to 'pluck the cherry' and now there was no cherry to be plucked.

"I'm still a virgin but I might not bleed when you...you know..."

For a second I wondered if she had slept with someone else but even as the thought formed I dismissed it.

"You *do* believe me, don't you?" she asked, sounding hurt at my silence.

"Of course, I do," I reassured her.

She's 5'5" but when I wrapped my arms around her and kissed her, she felt tiny. I'd never realized just how small she was. It made me even more worried. I kissed my way down her long neck, the sexy hollow in her shoulder, to the tops of her firm breasts. Her nipples were already erect by the time I got to them but my cock was so hard I was afraid to suck on one of them in case I came instantly. I rolled them between my fingers and felt my cock jerk between our bodies, anyway.

I'm going to cum before I get my cock inside her, I just know it! This thought ran through my head as I reached over to grab a condom.

Damn! I had left them on my writing desk near the door. Now I would have to walk naked with my cock in the air to retrieve them.

"I have to put on a condom," I whispered to her, got off the bed and grabbed the box.

I had already turned to walk back to the bed when I decided it might have been better to put the condom on, facing away from her. Then again, maybe not! Though it was embarrassing to walk back to the bed with my erection in the air, at least I blended into the darkness of the room— the condom would have practically glowed in the dim light!

I sat on the end of the bed, extracted a condom and ripped the packet with my teeth. I awkwardly rolled it in place, painfully aware that Angel was watching my every move.

She laughed softly, a little nervously, as I joined her under the duvet again, covering her body with mine. I kissed her, so aroused I pushed my tongue deep into her mouth, more deeply than I had ever done before. Eventually I broke the kiss, sucked on her neck and then pulled one of her nipples into my mouth. I never really lost my love of sucking on a nipple, when she arched her back, pressing her breast against my mouth, I immediately sucked harder. Remembering that Raymond had placed my hand between Geraldine's legs, I ran my hand up the smooth inside of Angel's and touched her pussy. It was covered with soft hair, everything neatly enclosed within her outer lips, unlike Geraldine's whose inner lips had curled outwards. I had almost instantly found Geraldine's prominent clitoris, I had to hunt for Angel's. I moved my lips to her other nipple as I opened her pussy lips, found her small clitoris and rubbed it firmly as I had done Geraldine's. Her whole body jerked and she screamed.

"Sorry!" I apologized, mortified.

"It's okay. Just do it gently, I am very sensitive down there." I hesitated, afraid of doing it wrong again but she covered my hand with hers and pleaded, "Touch me, Tariq."

I touched her lightly. She sighed and said, "Don't stop."

I sucked on her nipple and continued. I knew she was enjoying it by the way she was lifting her hips and rotating her pussy against my hand. It took a while but finally she pressed harder against my fingers and came with a soft moan.

Relieved that I had made her cum, I stopped worrying about cumming too quickly. I had put my finger inside her while fingering her clitoris and her opening had seemed quite tight. I slid down her body, opened her pussy and looked at her.

"Tariq!" She was scandalized but didn't try to close her legs.

My eyes confirmed what I had feared—her entrance was small—there was no way I could get my cock inside it without doing both of us serious injury.

"I'm not sure that I will fit inside you," I told her as I slid up the bed and lay next to her.

"Don't be silly, Tariq!" she reprimanded. "Babies come out of there, of course you can fit in."

She wanted to be a mid-wife, was fascinated with child-birth and babies—hence the baby analogy.

"Maybe I'm too tall for you," I said stupidly. Geraldine was taller and had a much bigger frame. Maybe Angel's vagina was in proportion to her tiny frame.

"Maybe you don't want to make love to me." Angel pouted. "Maybe you're just trying to find an excuse."

"Of course, I want to make love to you!" I retorted in surprise. "Why would you think that?"

"Because you never wanted to before," she complained and suddenly started crying.

Not dainty tears but big noisy sobs.

"Of course I want to make love to you." I pressed my rigid cock against her so she could feel how much I wanted her, just as the door knob turned. I barely managed to pull the sheet up over her breasts before Raymond pushed the door open and switched on the lights.

"Angel, are you alright?" he demanded, giving me a dirty look.

"I'm fine, Ray." She gave him a weak smile.

"Okay." He backed out and left.

"Sorry, Tariq!" she apologized, embarrassed. "I didn't know he'd hear me."

"Don't worry about it—the walls are as thin as paper."

"Can you lock the door?"

"He won't come back," I promised. I had never locked the door, wasn't even sure if it could be locked.

"Please."

"OK." I got off the bed, with my hard cock in the air, again, pulled the safety lock downwards and hurried back to the bed.

As I was about to lie on top of her, she pushed against my chest. "Maybe it will be easier if I was on top."

I lay back, supported by a couple of pillows and the headboard. She swung her leg over me, kneeling astride my waist, my cock behind her, resting against her ass. She placed her small hands on my chest and lifted herself up and onto the head of my cock. I immediately pressed upwards.

"Wait!" She stopped me from thrusting upwards again, reaching between us to position my cock correctly.

It was obvious that my cock had no sense of direction— it hadn't been able to find Geraldine's entrance without help either.

Angel sank slowly onto me in small increments, moving herself up and down, her pussy gripping me tightly but not too painfully. She never looked more beautiful to me: her full lips parted, her hair in disorder, her slim shoulders tense as she supported some of her body weight on her arms, her breasts pushed forward, her small nipples erect.

I let go of her hips and cupped her breasts, pulling her closer to wrap my mouth around one of her hard nipples. I tried to hold on until she came again but almost as soon as the last of my cock disappeared from view inside her, I came with a smothered groan.

I pulled her down to lie against my chest and almost immediately I was ready again. I reversed our positions, my cock still inside her. She held my gaze as I withdrew slowly, almost completely but as I slid inside her again she winched, bit her bottom lip and turned her head to the side.

I paused, cupped her face and turned her head so that she was facing me again. "Do you want me to stop?"

"Not really."

Not really? Was that a yes or no?

"I can stop if you want me to." I didn't really want to leave her nice, snug pussy but I didn't want to hurt her either.

"I'm just a little sore," she admitted.

I eased myself out of her, grabbed my towel off the floor and said, "I'll be right back."

In the bathroom I whipped the condom off and took my cock in hand. It had been anticipating another session or two, there was no way it would deflate by itself so I quickly jerked myself off, standing over the bathtub. I leaned against the cool tiles for a few seconds before wiping myself with the flannel I'd used earlier. Washing down the evidence from the bathroom walls, I hurried back to the bedroom.

Angel had snuggled under the covers, leaving just her face visible. She looked like a sleepy ten-year-old. Laughing, I pulled the duvet back and she gave a groan of protest.

"Don't you want to come for a quick shower?" I asked, bending to scoop her out of the bed.

"I'm too sleepy," she complained.

"Okay, stay here. I'll give you a wash."

Grabbing the towel I had planned to use to catch the 'cherry' blood, I raced to the bathroom and dampened the end of it, using fairly hot water.

It was still pleasantly warm when I ran it over Angel's chest and between her legs. Tossing it in the direction of my computer chair, I slipped under the duvet and pulled her into my arms.

It took me a while to fall asleep.

I kept replaying the events of the night over and over again in my head. I had left Geraldine's reeling with disappointment after giving Raymond head—neither of us had enjoyed the experience and it had left me feeling even more confused about my sexuality. I had enjoyed Edwin giving me head but Geraldine's expert mouth had given me as much pleasure. I had felt no compulsion to fuck Edwin's ass again but I had eagerly fucked Geraldine's as a means of being closer to Raymond. Finally, I'd had a chance to get up close and personal with Raymond's cock and it had been an anti-climax. And then the very thing I had feared; had desperately tried to avoid—making love to Angel—had turned out to be more emotionally intense than I had expected. I had almost screamed the second before cumming, her pussy wrapped tightly around my cock, her nipple in my mouth. *That* moment had bordered on perfection.

***

I woke up with her snuggled up close to me, my morning erection squashed between us. I turned to look at the alarm clock and the towel that I'd used to wipe her off caught my eye. There was blood on it—not a lot but enough to make my heart beat faster. I pulled the duvet back cautiously, expecting to find her lying in a pool of blood.

Nothing. Thank God!

But I had definitely taken her virginity. I was surprised at the emotion that rushed through me. I hadn't thought that I had doubted her until that very moment. I felt ashamed of my joy but I couldn't contain it. I hugged her even tighter and went back to sleep.

We woke up around midday and she sneaked out of the bedroom, wearing my bathrobe. She bumped into Raymond on her way back from the bathroom and rushed back into the room looking shy.

We made love again when we finally went to bed at two the next morning after watching two rented DVDs with

Raymond. Well, not made love exactly, she was still sore so I fingered her and sucked on her nipples until she came and then she stroked my cock until I did. Later the next afternoon I gave her a lift home. Her mother gave me a stern look when I walked into her living room but I greeted her politely and made my exit as soon as I could.

On a whim I decided to visit Geraldine.

Her mouth dropped open when she opened the door and found me standing on her doorstep. I almost heard the sound of her ass clenching instinctively.

"Tariq, *what* are you doing here?"

"I brought you a belated birthday present," I explained, pulling the bunch of roses that I'd bought at a roadside florist from behind my back and giving them to her. "I also came to say goodbye and thank you for everything."

"You *did* pay me, honey," she reminded me as she ushered me inside.

"I know but I still feel bad about having anal sex with you," I apologized.

I'd had to overrule my gentlemanly instincts to have anal sex with her sensing that she wasn't enjoying it and knowing that I was causing her some discomfort. But it had seemed a necessary evil at the time. If I'd made love to Angel months before, maybe…

"Don't worry about it, honey. It's part of the job."

It was only then that I noticed the young woman lying on the couch, her erect nipples poking through her thin top as though someone had just been sucking or teasing them. I looked back at Geraldine and realized that she wasn't her usual well-groomed self. They must have been rolling around on the couch before I'd pressed the doorbell. Raymond and I had wondered if the young woman, Tiffany, was Geraldine's daughter. Obviously *not!*

"Would you like a drink?" Geraldine asked.

"No, I have to get back." I turned at the door and winked at her. "And *you* have to get back to Tiffany!"

Her laughter followed me to my jeep.

***

Raymond and I are now thirty-one. We don't hang out as much as we used to, due to work and family commitments, but we are still good friends. We have never discussed the night I'd risked irrevocably damaging our friendship but occasionally I look at him and feel a tiny flicker of the flame that has lain dormant for years.

Angel and I got married just after she qualified as a midwife and we now have a seven-month old son. The little scamp and I fight constantly for Angel's attention. I had been considering giving him up for adoption and not having any more kids until we visited my parents recently.

The little rascal had been breast-feeding, looking at me smugly, deliberately taunting me with his chubby hand on my wife's breast. He could afford to be smug, he was winning the battle for Angel's breasts and it had been that way since he was born. He had latched on to a nipple as soon as he had drawn breath and showed no sign of giving up in the foreseeable future.

I complained to my parents that Angel was spoiling him and that it was time he stopped breast-feeding.

My father had laughed and said, "Now you see how *I* felt."

It had taken a moment for me to realize what he was talking about. Then I'd laughed my ass off—I'd completely forgotten my almost three year reign at my mother's breasts.

Raymond, my son's godfather, always said the little devil is a chip off the old block!

***

As teenagers, most of us experience an attraction for someone of the same sex, although we may not be homosexual. Boys are usually more worried about these feelings; girls tend to view them as part of the growing up process and let time be the deciding factor.

I wrote this story for a close friend of mine who once confessed to me that he'd had a massive crush on his best friend when he was about fifteen. He outgrew his crush and is now happily married with kids but has always wondered how his life would have turned out if he had been bold enough to tell his friend how he felt or if his friend had felt the same way about him.

*****

SHAWN 'THE DOG' MITCHELL

Stuck in the holiday traffic on the way to his great-aunt May's house, Shawn cursed himself for being a mummy's boy. His mother had called him three days ago from Martinique, concerned about her aunt who was spending the first Christmas on her own since the death of her husband. Neither of his sisters was available: the older one was heavily pregnant with her fourth child, and his parents had taken the younger on holiday with them. So, reluctantly he had agreed to drive down late Christmas Eve and spend Christmas Day and part of Boxing Day with his great-aunt. He had thought his new girlfriend Loretta would come along to keep him company. Instead, she had quickly logged on to the Internet and found a last-minute flight to Florida to spend the holidays over there with her best friend. Worst of all was the fact that she had finally uncrossed her legs last Friday after two months of roses, expensive dinners and endless begging. He had been 'hitting' her pussy with a vengeance every night since and had planned to 'bend' it up during his two week Christmas vacation.

Fucking hell! The first Christmas in four years that he could drink and be merry, without the prospect of exams in

January hanging over his head since he'd achieved a MEng in Civil Engineering and he had lost his Xmas pussy and had to look after an old lady.

Still wishing that he was the kind of bastard son who could have refused his mother's request and not felt bad, he turned his Peugeot 306 into the driveway of his great-aunt's neat two-bedroom end-of-terrace house.

The front door opened and a slim figure rushed out to greet him as he turned the engine off. He got out the car and opened his arms to hug her. She leaned back in his embrace and smiled up at him, "Hi, baby."

"Aunt May! What have you been doing to yourself?"

She had always looked good for her age but it was as if she had taken twenty years off since he had last seen her.

"I know I look good but close your mouth, boy!"

"I came here expecting to find a sad, lonely old lady and what do I find instead—a happy, smiling woman who looks too young even to be my mother!"

"I told your mother I was fine but she wouldn't listen to me."

Damn! He had given up his Xmas pussy for nothing!

***

"Do you miss Uncle Sidney?" he asked her on Christmas Day as they sat sipping Johnny Walker Gold Label, her late husband's favourite tipple.

"I do, baby, especially the sex."

"Aunt May!"

"Boy, don't act like I am too old for sex. Only last week I had to pay my boy-toy to come over and see to my needs."

"I don't want to hear this!" Shawn protested, horrified.

"Oh shut up!" She reached over and pinched his cheek. "I hope you don't object to him coming over tomorrow evening."

"Aunt May, I am leaving tomorrow afternoon, so it

doesn't matter. But even if I had planned on staying longer I would have left anyway—I couldn't be in the house while you had some stranger on top of you."

"You could always slip into the wardrobe and peep like you did when you were younger."

"H-how…?" Shawn spluttered.

"Boy, please! You were breathing so hard I had to make extra noise so that your uncle wouldn't hear you! He was a very jealous man. If he knew that you had seen me naked he would have packed your clothes and sent you back to spend Christmas in that big house all by yourself."

At 5'2" Aunt May had the same slim, neat body that Shawn's grandmother, his mother and older sister shared— small breasts, trim waist, rounded behinds and well-shaped legs. Many of his school friends had come over to his house on some pretext or other just to ogle his older sister. But once he had caught his best friend eyeing his mother's behind and he had almost flattened him. Leering at his sister was bad enough, lusting after his mother was a declaration of war! Shawn's younger sister, like him, had inherited their father's height. She had also studied karate since the age of seven and now at eighteen was still a tomboy—none of his friends had ever thought of messing with her, much to his relief.

"I can't believe you knew that I was in the wardrobe!" He was shocked shitless by his great-aunt's revelation. "Why didn't you say something before?"

"Why should I? I didn't mind at all! When I was a young girl I used to peep at my mother and father making love all the time. We were so poor your grandmother and I shared the same bedroom with them. When they thought we'd gone to sleep, they would start. Your grandmother always slept through it but I used to raise the edge of my sheet and watch them do it under the covers. My father was a tall man and I think he had a big penis; my mother was barely five foot—he had the devil's own job getting it inside her!"

Shawn vaguely remembered his great-grandmother, he was seven when she'd died suddenly but he remembered that she'd been very petite. His great-grandfather still lived in Barbados. The last time he had gone to the island to spend the summer holidays as a five-foot-ten, sixteen-year-old, his great-grandfather had still topped his height by an inch or two even though his carriage had begun to stoop with age.

"How could you watch your parents make love?" he asked incredulously. Although he knew that it was unlikely, he always hoped that his father wasn't still messing with his mother. Now Aunt May had given him even more to worry about—his slender mother was over a foot shorter than his solidly-built father.

"Girls are far more realistic than boys. We understand that our parents make love for pleasure; *you* probably think that your parents did it only to make children and stopped once they had your little sister."

He laughed as Aunt May accurately guessed his thoughts. "You're right. I just don't like to think of any man doing to my mother what I do to my girlfriends, not *even* my father."

"Believe me if your mother is anything like me, you should worry about your father, not *her*!"

"How much do you pay this young man?" he asked, changing the subject before Aunt May revealed something about his parents' sex life that would send him into shock or a mental institution.

"I pay him £100 for two hours or £200 to spend the night."

"What?"

"He's worth every penny. My friends think so too."

"*What?*" he was so shocked he forgot that he was talking

to an older relative as he continued, "He *fucks* your friends too?"

"Isabel, Mavis, Carmen and Pamela have all lost their husbands too. We each have a bit of money but nothing to spend it on except bingo. Isabel has a son whom she hasn't seen in twenty years but the rest of us have no children or grandchildren. We call ourselves 'The Merry Widows'." May laughed. "About four months ago Isabel confessed that she'd paid him to spend the night on her birthday and she'd had a good time. The other ladies called him straight away but I wasn't sure that I wanted some young man getting on top of me, but I finally called him three weeks ago when I was feeling a little lonely after a few glasses of wine."

"How often does he come over?"

"He's only been over to see me twice before, he is a big boy and the first time I needed a fortnight to recover. Last week was much better and I am ready for another seeing-to."

"I hope you use protection!"

"Of course I do! I am not senile yet."

"I can't imagine you paying some young man money to *jump* your bones."

"Well now that I've given you back your money you could give me another present instead."

Shawn hadn't gotten a chance to buy her a present, so he had stopped on the way over, bought her a Christmas card and put some money inside before sealing it, thinking that his great-aunt might be finding it hard to make ends meet since her husband had died of a stroke earlier in the year. Instead she had slipped the money back into his pocket and told him that she had received substantial payouts from her husband's previous employer as well as the insurance company Sidney had paid hefty premiums each month religiously to ensure that she was well-provided for in the event of his death.

"What kind of present are we talking about?" he asked cautiously.

"Boy, stop beating around the bush! You know that I want you to see to my needs."

"Aunt May, Mum would kill me!"

"Are you going to tell her?" she challenged.

His friends had nicknamed him 'The Dog' because he fucked anything that moved and was female. He had once fucked a woman and both of her daughters at the same time. He had met the younger daughter first and had officially dated her in the six months that the family had used him as a stud. He had never met a more competitive family. The mother had barely spoken two words to him when he had gone to her house to visit her daughter the first time. Yet, two days later he had come home to find her waiting for him in her car. Convinced that she'd been there to voice her disapproval of him, he'd reluctantly invited her inside. It had come as a complete shock when she'd dropped to her knees in front of him and freed his cock. She hadn't even wanted to let it go long enough for him to put on a condom but he had insisted. Her elder sister had been a little more subtle, dropping hints—even in front of her sister—until the day she had called him and told him that her sister wasn't good enough for him. She had come over to his flat less than half an hour later to prove that she was better than her sister.

Shawn had also fucked many of his girlfriends' *so-called* friends. He didn't know what it was about girlfriends—why they felt the need to tell their friends how well he fucked them. All it did was rouse jealousy in their friends' breasts. They would then somehow manage to get his telephone number, home or work address and come to prove to him that he was dating the wrong friend. Dog that he is, he usually fucked them, if they were fine, and then dogged them by staying with his girlfriend. He wasn't stupid enough to make a woman, who had slept with him knowing that he was her friend's man, his main squeeze.

He had also slept with a few of his friends' girlfriends. His defence was that maybe a few of his friends had slept with his girlfriends too—he was good looking but so were most of his friends. Some of them owned costly properties, had better jobs and drove more expensive cars, why not?

But this was too much! Aunt May was family! Even if she looked incredible for her age.

"Aunt May, I couldn't!" he protested, his cock as hard as a rock.

"Okay, I'll call my young man but you are not going anywhere until the New Year. Your mother told me that you're off for two weeks, you'll stay here and keep me company."

***

Crawling under the duvet later that night he remembered his aunt's words, '*You could always slip into the wardrobe and peep...*'

His face burned as he recalled the Christmas he had spent with her and her husband when he was thirteen years old. His mother and father had gone on a cruise to celebrate his father's 35th birthday. His two sisters had gone to stay with his father's sister but he had decided to stay with May.

They had eaten a lavish Christmas dinner and he had been sent to bed at midnight. He had been playing Tetris on his Gameboy when his great-aunt and Sidney had come up to bed half an hour later. Immediately he started hearing strange noises. Pressing his ear against the wall, he had heard May urging her husband on, "Give it to me now!"

He'd heard Sidney tell her, "Darling, be quiet, the boy's sleeping next door", but his aunt had carried on, "Yes, give it to me nice and deep...don't hold back...give me everything you've got."

His mind had run riot at the images her voice had evoked. The next evening he had slipped into the built-in wardrobe in their bedroom and hid until they came up stairs.

He had watched through the slightly open door as his uncle had quickly undressed May and knelt on the floor in front of her. She had hooked a leg over his shoulder and he had eaten her pussy to his great-aunt's loud and obvious enjoyment. The only problem for Shawn was that she had put up the leg nearest to him and had effectively blocked his view of the action. He had contended himself with admiring her petite body. At the time she had been in her early-forties but her body had been that of a teenaged girl. She'd never had any children, no one knew if the problem lay with her or her husband or if they had both decided against it, neither of them had ever breathed a word to anyone outside their marriage.

He had watched in amazement as May's husband had straightened and lifted his wife up and onto his erect cock. Wrapping her legs around his waist, she had started a gyration that quickly buried his cock inside her.

"God, May, you're so sweet!" Her husband had sounded as though he was in pain but May had kept up her gyrations, moaning quite loudly as she did so.

Suddenly Sidney's knees had started to buckle. He had staggered back and sat heavily down on the end of the bed. May had knelt on the bed, held onto his shoulders and bounced up and down on him. He had clamped his mouth around one of her nipples and she had ridden him furiously until they both came.

He had hitched himself up further on the bed, pulled the duvet over them and within minutes he had fallen asleep with her lying on top of him. Shawn had then slipped out of the wardrobe and headed for his bedroom.

The next day he caught his aunt looking strangely at him

several times but had been sure that there was no way she could have known that he had watched them—she had known for ten years and had never said a single word!

***

They spent Boxing Day quietly. First he helped her pack up some of her husband's things to give to charity. She told Shawn that she had been unable to complete the task on her own but with him there offering comfort, she didn't feel as sad. Then they looked through dozens of photo albums. Aunt May was the family's unofficial historian, she had pictures of all significant events that had occurred in the family and never went anywhere without her very expensive compact Nikon in her handbag.

At nine that evening the boy-toy rang the doorbell promptly. Shawn hurried to his room to avoid the embarrassment of meeting the man, probably no older than himself, who had come to 'see' to his aunt's needs as she put it.

He threw himself across the bed and wondered again why he had decided to stay on. He would have preferred being alone in his flat rather than being in the same house as his great-aunt and her paid stud.

He was on his feet and at the bedroom door before he realized it. Pushing all rational thought aside, he continued next door to his aunt's room. The antique wardrobe seemed to have shrunk. Belatedly he remembered that he had just become a teenager the last time he had hidden in it not the hulking 6'2" he now was.

The bedroom door opened a minute later and May walked in with the boy-toy. Austin Peterson, if he had given May and her friends his real name, looked nothing like the kind of man any woman would pay to have fuck her. He was about 5'8" and so skinny he looked anorexic.

He and May quickly shed their clothes.

"Miss May, I know that I've said this before but you have the body of a young girl."

Shawn knew that it was probably a line the man fed to all his customers but he had to agree with him. May's shoulder-length, unprocessed hair was peppered with beautiful silvery grey strands but time had stood still when it came to her body. He didn't know if it was purely good genes or the hour of yoga she practised every day. She climbed onto the bed while the young man rolled a condom onto his average-sized erection.

Aunt May thought Austin was a big boy? *I'd better not show her mine!*

Austin climbed onto the bed and stretched out beside May. He reached over and grabbed the tube of lubricant that Aunt May must have put there in readiness. He squeezed some onto his fingers and May opened her legs as he brought his hand downwards. He smeared the moisture over her pussy, then reached for the tube again. This time he slid the fingers inside her. "I want you nice and wet. You bruised my cock the last time and put me out of action the next day."

"I'm sorry about that, honey. I'll give you a little extra to make it up to you."

"Don't get me wrong, Miss May," Mr Anorexia told her. "I enjoy a tight pussy as much as the next man but in my line of business it's an occupational hazard."

He bent his head and took the nipple of one of May's small still firm breasts into his mouth as he continued to finger-fuck her. May had, in the meantime, wrapped her hand around his cock and was stroking it up and down.

"I think you are ready now." He sat up and knelt between May's thighs. "Rub some lubricant on it for me, Miss May."

Aunt May picked up the still-open tube, applied a line of

moisture directly onto the condom, capped the tube and then rubbed the moisture along the condom.

Austin lowered himself between her legs and braced himself on his arms.

"Ready, Miss May?"

"Whenever you are, honey."

He entered her with a quick, deep thrust and Shawn heard his aunt groan. Not giving her time to adjust, he started to alternatively withdraw and plunge his cock with no fucking style as far as Shawn was concerned.

That's why his cock gets sore!

Shawn was sure that the man had taken something as he continued to pound away at May's pussy. He didn't try to kiss her and he dipped his head only twice to briefly flick his tongue at a nipple during his onslaught.

When he decided that it was time for May to cum, he stopped his mechanical thrusting, took one of her nipples into his mouth and stroked her clit. May stiffened, her toes pointing as she came loudly.

"I love the way you cum, Miss May." Austin pulled himself out of her without cumming himself.

"Honey-child, shush your mouth!"

May grabbed some tissues from the box on the bedside table and pulled the condom off Austin. He lay back and May snuggled into his bony arms. He idly fondled the cheeks of her ass before running a finger down the crack.

"Boy, don't play around my asshole!" May slapped his hand away.

"I am telling you Miss May you don't know what you are missing!"

"I am too old a dog to be taught new tricks."

"Miss May, you are as young as the man you're feeling and right now you're feeling me."

Shawn rolled his eyes.

The man was simple and couldn't fuck. How could his aunt tolerate him!

"Would you like something to drink?" May asked as she sat up.

"I'll have another shot of your Hennessey."

Aunt May pulled on a robe and left the room.

As soon as the door closed behind her the skinny fucker leaned over and opened the top drawer of her bedside table. He opened her purse and quickly pulled out a £50 note. He slipped it into his jeans pocket and lay back on the bed just as Aunt May came in with a fat tumbler containing a generous amount of the amber liquid.

"Thanks, Miss May," he said as he took the glass from her. "A few sips of this and I'll be ready to fuck your tight pussy again."

Fucking bastard! Shawn felt like coming out of the wardrobe and kicking the shit out of the anorexic thief.

"Ready for this big boy again?" Austin asked her, stroking his cock.

"Yes, sweetheart."

"This time, Miss May, I want you to ride me like I am your favourite pony."

He lay back with his stiff cock standing to attention. Aunt May rubbed some lubricant onto the fresh condom he had rolled on and climbed onto him. She positioned herself against his cock and rotated her hips until it was buried inside her. She leaned over and pushed one of her nipples into his mouth and then started a series of gyrations that made Shawn's cock instantly harden again.

Aunt May hadn't lost any of her skills.

Austin moved his lips to May's other nipple as she quickened her movements. She moaned aloud as she came again, completely drowning out the young man's softer groans as he came too.

She collapsed on top of him and they lay together for a few moments. Finally as his deflating cock started to slip out of May's pussy, she sat up and pulled herself off him.

Reaching into her drawer she took out her purse and peeled some notes off.

"Here's £100 for today and another £100 because I made you lose work after you were here the last time."

"Miss May, you are too generous!"

Yeah, but you didn't refuse it, you slimy toad!

"Do you mind if I leave a little early?"

Shawn looked at the luminous hands of his watch. Austin had only been there for forty-five minutes—two hundred and fifty pounds for less than an hour of bad fucking! Incredible!

"You go right ahead, honey." May hugged him briefly. "I'm fine until the next time."

Austin pulled on his T-shirt and jeans as May pulled back on her robe. As soon as they left the room, Shawn came out the wardrobe and sat on the bed to await May's return.

"So, what did you think of my *boy-toy*?" she asked as she re-entered the room, showing no surprise at finding him there.

"He's a *bloody* thief!"

"Did he help himself to another £50 note?" May's lack of surprise shocked Shawn as she casually walked over to the table and picked up her purse. She quickly counted the remaining notes. "He's not a greedy boy; some men would have taken more."

"You *know* that he steals from you?" Shawn questioned, shocked.

"I left my purse there the last time to see if he would be tempted. As soon as he left I counted my money and realized that he had taken a £50 note. He wants to start his own business soon, so I don't mind him taking the extra money."

"Aunt May, the man can't even fuck properly!"

"He is young; he'll get better as he gets older."

"I can't believe that you pay *him* £50 an hour! All I get after four years of university and an upper second class degree is a measly £28 an hour!"

"Well, I gave you first choice and you turned it down."

He tried to ignore her last statement. His cock was still hard, and standing in front of him with her robe gaping, his great-aunt was too much of a temptation.

"Aunt May what you need is a good vibrator or dildo."

"Honey, you can't wrap your arms around a dildo."

The words were uttered lightly but for the first time he realized that she was lonely. Sidney had been a loving husband and they had constantly hugged and kissed each other. He had even heard his mother once complain that they behaved like teenagers. He remembered the way she had crawled into the boy's bony arms and felt inexplicably sad for her.

"I can give you a hug any time you need one." He pulled her close and wrapped his arms around her. Though he was sitting on the bed her head rested comfortably on his shoulder. He held her for as long as he dared before getting off the bed and heading for the door, mumbling that he was going to grab a shower through clenched teeth.

He needed a *very* cold one.

The next day all he could think of every time he looked at May was her riding the young man's cock like a seasoned cowgirl. It was definitely time to go back to his empty flat.

"Aunt May, I'm leaving in the morning," he informed her as they sat down to dinner later that evening.

"Honey, can't you stay another week? You said your girlfriend's in Florida, why are you going back to an empty flat?"

"I've got some work to—"

"Don't give me that excuse. I saw you fetch your laptop inside when you arrived."

"God, Aunt May, you don't miss a trick!"

"You're staying right here and that's the end of it."

***

Shawn spent the next few days helping May around the house. Doing a few *man* things that were too trivial for her to pay a professional to do but needed doing anyway: like changing the lock on the storeroom door, putting up hooks so that she could hang even more of the photographs she had taken, etc.

The Merry Widows came over to play bridge the next evening.

Shawn developed a grudging respect for the anorexic Austin. The man could fuck anything, he was even more *dog* than Shawn. Isabel was a bony woman in her mid-fifties who Shawn couldn't fuck for all the money in the world. Mavis was late sixties and though it was believed that beauty faded over the years, it was obvious that she'd never had any to begin with. Pamela was sixty going on sixteen. The stingy fucker she had married had subjected the poor woman to a life of charity shop clothing and marked down or expired food. When he had died the large amount of money in his bank account had almost given her a heart attack, but even before she had put him in the ground she had started to splurge. She had no sense of style, buying sexy outfit after sexy outfit, suited for women half her age and size. Her husband had only ever visited Sainsbury's or Tesco supermarkets for bargains, considering them too expensive. With her newfound wealth Pamela considered them too cheap, she bought only Marks & Spencer foods, and lots of it. She had doubled her body mass in the two years since her husband's death and seem bent on tripling it by the third anniversary. She deserved a sympathy fuck for the tough life she'd had but Shawn wasn't _that_ sympathetic.

Carmen was forty-seven, almost six foot and about two hundred pounds. The dog in Shawn sat up and howled at the sight of her. She had quite a sexy figure: full chest, trim waist, huge butt and massive thighs. Thighs that could crush all the bones in a man's face if he pissed her off or got her too excited while he was eating her pussy. He definitely wouldn't put his head between her legs when he fucked her. Which was only a matter of time. He was 'The Dog', after all.

***

"Can I get you ladies another drink?" Shawn asked politely.

"Yes, please," Pamela and Mavis responded immediately.

"May, this young man has such nice manners." Isabel winked at him and said, "I'll have another gin and milk, please."

"Gin and milk?" Shawn queried. Is that what the mess in her glass was? "Skimmed, semi-skimmed or whole?"

"Evaporated," Carmen offered and stood up, "I'll help you get them."

Shawn recognized Carmen's offer for the blatant sexual invitation it was. As soon as they entered the kitchen, he pulled her against him. Her Amazonian curves filled his arms and she smelled amazing. He cupped her butt and rubbed his cock against her.

"Give me your address and I'll come over later," he whispered in her ear, reluctantly letting her go to fix the drinks before his aunt came looking for them.

Carmen tore a page off May's shopping list pad and used the attached pen to quickly scribble her address.

"I'll make an excuse and leave early," she promised.

Half an hour later, as soon as a game ended, Carmen

stood up and said, "I think I'll leave early tonight. I want to check on my mother on the way home."

"How is she doing?" May asked concerned.

"As well as can be expected."

Shawn chatted to Pamela as May saw Carmen to her car. The other ladies left an hour and a half later.

"I think I'll go up to bed," Shawn told his great-aunt, stifling a fake yawn.

***

Carmen came to the door wearing a sheer black wrapper, her nipples poking through the material. Shawn kicked the door shut with his foot as he took her into his arms.

"Tell me what you like. I'm here for your pleasure."

"Anything?" she queried.

"Anything," he promised.

"My husband was a breast man, since he died I haven't had someone suck on my nipples properly; Austin is a bit too rough for my liking. I have several toys that I use to keep myself happy but no one to take care of my nipples like my husband used to."

"I can take care of them, all night if you want me to."

"Would you?"

He knelt on the soft rug beside her bed and freed her breasts.

"I will," he vowed as he squashed her soft breasts together and circled her pouting nipples with his tongue. "Carmen, you taste delicious."

"Dear sweet Jesus!" she moaned as he took her big nipples into his mouth and gently sucked on them both at the same time. She reached between them and slid two fingers into her pussy and said, "Suck on them a bit harder, baby."

He obliged and a tremor ran through her body. He kept up his insistent tugging until she gave a groan and pulled her fingers out. "You're making me so horny, baby! I think I'll need you to fuck me as well."

"Carmen, those are some of the sweetest words I've ever heard."

Shawn quickly whipped a condom out of his pocket and pulled it on. Nudging her legs further apart, he pushed her back onto the bed and plunged his eager cock into her wet pussy. She wasn't tight—she must use *very* big toys—but there was enough friction to keep him happy. He cupped her breasts and sucked alternately on her nipples as he thrust into her deeply, withdrawing the full length of his cock and plunging it smoothly back inside her.

It's a shame the other widows are so old, Shawn thought as he sneaked back into his Aunt May's house just before dawn, *I could have made them all merry.*

***

The next morning he walked into the kitchen at eight-thirty to find his aunt cooking an English breakfast: mushrooms, salad tomatoes, prime sausages, organic eggs and thick-cut bacon.

"Aunt May, you know the way to a man's heart." Shawn waited until she had taken a sunny-side up egg from the pan before hugging her from behind.

"I thought you would need to replenish the energy you used up last night."

"Aunt May, what are you talking about? I slept like a log."

"Boy, I wasn't born yesterday! Carmen suddenly having to check on her sick mother…you suddenly going to bed early…it was as obvious as the nose on your face. Plus I heard you coming in this morning while I was doing my Yoga stretches."

Busted!

"You were doing Yoga at five-fifteen in the morning?"

"I am usually up at five every morning doing my Yoga but since you've been here I read for an hour or two before getting up so that I don't disturb you."

"I-I—," Shawn couldn't think of an appropriate excuse.

"Eat your breakfast while it's hot and stop trying to make up lame excuses."

Shawn jumped up onto a stool at his aunt's breakfast bar and she passed him a loaded plate.

"This looks real good, Aunt May," he complimented, before diving in.

***

On New Year's Eve he and Aunt May watched the fireworks display at Trafalgar Square on television and then listened to some music before going up to bed.

He was lying on his back wondering what Loretta was getting up to when his bedroom door opened and Aunt May slipped into the room.

"I don't want to be alone tonight," she explained before lifting the edge of the duvet and slipping under it.

He pulled her close and spooned her from the back.

His hand itched to slip under the lace of her nightgown, cup her breast and tweak her nipple but he kept it on her waist. His cock refused to be controlled, it hardened and bridged the gap he had left between their bodies, poking into her ass. She rolled over and faced him, pressing her front along the length of his without saying a word.

Well, he had tried *not* being 'The Dog' but there was only so much a man could take!

He kissed her deeply as he slid the straps of her nightgown off her shoulders to reveal her small breasts. Both nipples were standing to attention. Bending his head, he covered one with his lips, circling it repeatedly with his tongue, until May pressed his mouth firmly against her and commanded, "Boy, stop teasing me!"

He immediately pulled most of her breast into his mouth. In response she undulated her slim body against his and leaned down to rain kisses along the side of his face. He cupped her pussy before pushing the gusset of her panty aside and stroking her clit—she was slick with her own juices.

Why the fuck had Austin used all that damned lubricant? Shawn had heard that older women's pussies were dry, not his Aunt May's. He shifted his hips as he felt her trying to slip her hand into his boxers. She reached inside and wrapped her hand around him.

"Whoa!" She pushed the duvet back and reached over to switch on the reading lamp. "Damn, boy! Carmen actually let you stick this thing inside her?"

Shawn laughed but didn't answer. He couldn't tell his aunt that the youngest of the Merry Widows had some serious hardware at her disposal and had taken the full length of his cock with no trouble.

"You must get that from your great-grandfather," May said as she grasped it in both hands firmly. "I am sure he was a big boy too."

She bent her head to take it into her mouth and he groaned in anticipation. Though he felt like the world's biggest *dog*, he closed his eyes and grasped the pillows either side of his head as she wrapped her mouth around the head.

He kept his eyes closed as she continued. He usually liked to watch women give him head but he felt too embarrassed to watch his Aunt May go down on him. But instead of detracting from his pleasure, closing his eyes seemed to make the sensation of her mouth on him more intense. Within minutes he felt himself ready to cum.

He tried to pull away but May wouldn't let go.

"No, Aunt May!" he protested as the first stream of sperm shot into her mouth.

His aunt ignored him and kept swallowing until at last his cock stopped jerking.

"I wanted to swallow your cum, baby," she said as she finally released him. "It keeps me looking young and is so good for my complexion."

"I hope you don't go around swallowing men's cum *just* to stay young!"

"Of course I don't!"

"Aunt May, it's dangerous! You shouldn't have taken a chance with me—you don't know if I have AIDS or not!"

"Shawn, I have known you all your life—I doubt that you would sleep with a woman without using a condom."

Damn! She knew him so well, knew how fastidious he was.

"Aunt May, that's not the point!" he continued to berate her. "Condoms split sometimes you know! You shouldn't even be sleeping with Austin."

"I shouldn't be walking the street—I could be hit by a bus," his aunt replied flippantly.

"That's not the same and you know it."

"Baby, I know what you're saying and I'm grateful for your concern." She cupped his face and smiled at him. "For the record, I use the safest condoms on the market."

"I just don't like the idea of you having to pay some fool to come over and jump your bones. Especially one that does it so badly."

"Sidney and I had been making love since I was sixteen—it's a hard habit to break."

"Sixteen?" Shawn had lost his virginity at the same age to one of his older sister's friends but he was somehow appalled that Sidney had taken May's at the same age. "How old was Uncle Sidney?"

"Fifteen."

"I never knew he was younger than you!" He had always

thought that Sidney was at least ten years May's senior.

"Only by three months." May smiled as she said, "_I_ seduced him."

Without thinking any further, Shawn made a decision. "Aunt May we can't have sexual relations."

It wasn't fucking Aunt May that was the trouble; it was his mother finding out.

"That's okay, baby, I understand. Just hold me close."

"No, I don't mean that we are _done_," Shawn denied as he turned her over and started kissing his way down to her pussy. "I mean, Monica, that we will _not_ be having sexual relations."

"OK, Bill," his great-aunt laughed as she caught his meaning.

"Now, open your legs, and let me tongue this here pussy," he commanded and settled himself between her slim thighs as she parted them obediently.

Unlike the hair on her head, Aunt May's pubic hair was jet-black.

"Have you been dyeing these pussy hairs, Monica?"

"Boy, I'm old but not _that_ old!" May boxed his ears for his impertinence.

"Didn't mean to insult you, Monica," he apologized. "Let me shut up and just eat this pussy."

It had been a while since he had seen a pussy with its full covering of hair, Loretta like most young women shaved hers completely. It was strange to see a woman's pussy hidden under her pubic hair; to have to go diving to find her clit. He parted May's silky strands, ran his tongue along her inner lips and upwards to her clit.

"Boy, you have a wicked tongue!" Aunt May lifted herself to meet his lips as he put his mouth on her clit and ran his tongue over it firmly. "Damn, that's good!"

Shawn didn't have a problem going down on women,

weeks ago he had even tongued Loretta to a screaming orgasm through a dental dam, although she had informed him that she didn't really like oral sex. She hadn't returned the favour, yet he couldn't help but feel that she was one of those women who felt that a man wouldn't respect her if he thought she gave head. He wouldn't be at all surprised if one day she took his cock between her lips and gave him a blowjob to top all blowjobs. She was as sly as a fox. The first time they had made love she'd behaved as though she couldn't whiine, barely moving her hips as he thrust into her. By the next day it was as if she had taken an overnight course in waist-movement, rotating her hips so vigorously he'd had to literally pin her to the bed to keep from being thrown off. He honestly didn't know if he would call her when she got back from the States. In three nights of intensive fucking he had managed to get back most of the money he had invested in wining and dining her, he could move on now if he chose to. The only thing that would make him see her again was the possibility of the blowjob she might give him when she let her hair down further.

It was odd going down on a woman knowing that it wasn't just foreplay. He hadn't done it since his first girlfriend, yet he was surprised by his desire to make May feel extra good. When she came, he turned her over and kissed his way slowly from her toes, running his tongue over her insteps until she begged him to stop. He then bit her soft heels before moving on to the slim curves of her calves. He kissed, licked and nibbled the taut flesh of her butt before he opened the cheeks and rimmed her asshole. She nearly shot off the bed in surprise.

"Shawn, no!"

He bit her butt, then lifted his head briefly and said, "Don't worry, Monica, I am not an *ass* man, like Austin. I'm not even going to stick my finger inside you."

"You young people...the things you do," May's protests sounded as feeble as his had done earlier. He felt her raising her hips off the bed to press harder against his mouth. He continued for long moments as May squirmed and gasped. Finally she begged, "Shawn, stop! Stop now!"

He laughed as he moved up to kiss the small of her back, her shoulder and then her nape.

"Boy, where did you learn to eat pussy like that?"

"That's the way pussy is eaten in the 21st century, Monica, my dear. That's why you should get rid of Austin Fifty-pounds-an-hour-but-can't-fuck-to-save-his-fucking-life Peterson. You don't need him."

"Baby, you're right. I was only fooling myself that Austin's visits made me feel less lonely. I may as well find myself a nice old man and settle down instead of paying that boy my money."

"Not *too* old a man," Shawn warned. "You're too frisky a filly for an old stallion."

***

Shawn and May continued to *not* have sexual relations for the rest of the week and he was amazed how clear his conscience was when he left to go back to his own flat. She had promised to try dating a few of the old ferrets who had been queuing outside her door since Sidney's death, baying like wolves. Shawn had no doubt that she would soon find herself a nice guy to 'see' to her needs.

If Heaven forbid, his mother ever found out about him and May and asked him about it he would not feel like he was lying if he told her that he had never fucked May. His mother would give him a sound slap for cursing in front of her but it would be a small price to pay if it distracted her. He had once eavesdropped on a conversation between his mother and a rather plain-spoken Guyanese woman who lived two doors away from them in Balham. The woman had been playing away from home with another man but had told his mother that she hadn't been doing anything wrong because she and the man only engaged in oral sex, which she didn't personally consider to be real sex. His mother had disagreed but the woman had insisted, "Once cock ain't enter pussy—fuck ain't pass", meaning that she and the man hadn't been fucking because his penis hadn't entered her vagina.

Even at the age of fourteen, the woman's logic had made perfect sense to Shawn.

***

How close a relation is too close? I guess it is up to the individual but could you mess around with your aunt or great-aunt...even if she was very sexy?

If you cheated on your partner but only had oral sex, would you feel guilty? I think you definitely should, considering the fact that by doing so you are putting him or her at risk.

*****

EROTIC DREAMS

The huge black stallion sniffed the smaller mare's hindquarters, tossed his head arrogantly and snorted. She neighed encouragingly as he mounted her, his enormous penis jerking up and finding its mark with surprising accuracy. Her whinnying cries spurred him on as he proceeded to shove...

Shucks! Abigail sat up in bed crossly—something had awakened her in the middle of her favourite dream. She rubbed her eyes and slowly opened them as she listened to the sounds coming from her aunt's room. Odd noises interspersed with canine pants. She looked at her clock radio. It was five-twenty in the morning. Was that her aunt making odd noises? And why did Rover sound like he was out of breath? Or maybe it was Rover making all the noises. Maybe he needed to go out and her aunt was asleep.

She got out of bed and padded to her aunt's door. She tried the handle but the door was locked.

"What do you want?" her aunt demanded, her voice sounding strange.

"Aunt Imelda, I thought Rover wanted to go out."

"Rover's fine. Go back to bed."

"Okay, Auntie."

She returned to her bed, pulled the covers up to her neck and snuggled against the pillows. The sounds continued, softer but just as persistent. Then she heard her aunt whisper, "Good boy, good boy."

And then there was silence.

Abigail drifted off to sleep to be awakened by her aunt moving around the kitchen an hour later. She had a shower, put on a strapless sundress and joined her aunt for breakfast.

"I'm going into town to get some supplies," her aunt informed her as they cleared away the breakfast dishes. "Look out for the mailman but stay indoors until I come back."

"Yes, Auntie."

What her aunt really meant was: stay away from Frank, the farmhand. He was a huge lumbering young man who was considered a bit of an outcast in the village because he was the result of an affair between a fifteen-year-old Brazilian girl and a middle-aged British man. The girl's illiterate parents had both worked on the man's sheep farm and had been very grateful when he'd offered to school their young daughter, Maria. When she had become pregnant, the upright, church-going man had been the last person her parents had suspected. They had assumed that a local man had seduced her and she had refused to enlighten them. Unfortunately the baby boy had inherited his father's green eyes instead of his mother's amber ones. The man had paid the almost penniless parents a substantial amount, enough for them to turn a blind eye as he'd continued to fuck their young daughter. However, outraged villagers, some of them, it had to be said, a little jealous of the family's new financial status, reported the man to the police. The man had hastily obtained forged documents for his teenaged lover, married her and run back to Devon with his new bride and their young son.

On arrival in the UK he had been careful to disguise her extreme youth by ensuring that she wore make-up and sophisticated clothes. For years they'd had what seemed like a decent marriage until one cold December evening, Maria had shot her elderly husband through the head before turning the gun on herself, leaving sixteen-year-old Frank an orphan. His wealthy paternal grandfather, overcome with grief at the loss of his only child, hadn't needed a constant reminder of the woman who had taken his life, so he had sent Frank back to the Brazilian village with several thousand pounds and a one-way ticket, saying quite categorically that he never wanted to see him again. Sadly, Frank's maternal grandparents had also moved away soon after their daughter had left for the UK, leaving no forwarding address. When the young Frank had arrived he'd received a hostile reception from villagers who hadn't forgotten the scandal. That night Frank had returned to the farm which had once been owned by his father, sneaked up into the barn and spent the night.

Imelda Ramirez had bought the farm cheaply when Frank's father had been forced to flee. She was a tall, well-built woman who was considered a bit of an outcast herself—she had no husband or children and ran the large sheep farm almost single-handedly. Frank had been living in her barn for almost two weeks before she discovered him. She had noticed strange things on the farm—broken fences mended, pens mucked out, bales of hay she had piled haphazardly stacked neatly the next day, etc.

Then one evening, three years ago, she had been looking out her kitchen window when she had noticed a suspicious movement in the barn. She had gone to investigate and found the almost six-foot tall Frank stacking the hay that had been delivered earlier in the day. She had given him a job and allowed him to continue living in the barn. He effortlessly did the work of three men and she'd never regretted the day she'd hired him.

***

Abigail wished her aunt would stop treating her like she was a little girl. She was twenty-one years old, for heaven's sake! She understood her aunt's concerns, but she wasn't as naïve as her aunt thought. Though she had lived with her parents in an extremely remote part of the Amazon Jungle until six months ago when their Land Cruiser had overturned and killed them both, she knew the basics about sex and had secretly read the copy of the *Kama Sutra* her mother had kept hidden in a trunk. The book had cleared up several unanswered questions that had plagued her since she was seven years old and had sleepily gotten up to go to the bathroom in the middle of a swelteringly hot night. She had found the American representative from the company who funded her father's research sneaking in to the live-in maid's bedroom. On her way back from the bathroom she had heard them whispering and had innocently pushed the maid's bedroom door open to see what was going on. The maid had been kneeling on all-fours on the end of her single bed and the man, still fully dressed, had been standing behind her. Thinking that they were playing some kind of game, Abigail had climbed up onto the bed to join them.

The man had quickly pulled himself free. In the dim light Abigail had caught a quick glimpse of something protruding from his open fly before he'd rushed from the room. The maid had taken Abigail back to bed and tucked her in, making sure she was sound asleep before returning to her own room.

The next day Abigail had asked the maid what the man had been doing to her with the pink thing that had been hanging out of his trousers. The maid had told her that she had dreamt it. Abigail had believed her and hadn't questioned her further but years later on a weekend visit with her parents to a cattle ranch owned by a friend of her father's, she saw a stallion mount a mare. As she'd watched the stallion's penis disappear into the mare's hindquarters she'd had a flashback of the night she had interrupted the visitor from Maryland and their maid. The man had been mounting the maid and pushing his thing inside her. She was sure of it!

Abigail's parents had been botanists and sometimes on field trips with them she had seen monkeys mating high up in trees and wild boars mounting the stout backsides of bush pigs but the sheer size of the stallion's penis had astounded her. She spent the rest of the day thinking about it: wondering how it was possible for it to retract so completely into the animal's belly; how the mare had felt to have it inside her; did men's penises have the same ability to extend to such great lengths and if so, did it hurt when they pushed it up women's backsides?

In bed that night she had knelt on all-fours and reached behind to find an opening on her body that might be suitable for a man to push his *thing* into. She found none. There was no way a man could push his penis into her asshole, she couldn't get even her little finger inside it nor could he get it into her vagina. Maybe, she'd thought, they simply pushed it between the woman's legs and not into an opening.

Satisfied, she had gone to sleep, relieved that she had solved the mystery.

Years later the *Kama Sutra* dispelled her misconceptions.

***

Abigail hid behind the drapes and watched as Frank mowed her aunt's lawn. His damp shirt clung to the broad expanse of his back and his huge biceps rippled as he pushed the ancient mower over the lush grass.

Suddenly he straightened, cut the motor and wiped his brow. He returned the mower to the tool shed and then stood looking up towards the house, staring straight at the window. For a moment she thought he could see her. She felt the familiar tightening of her vaginal muscles before a hot flow of liquid drenched her panties. Just when she felt compelled to step from behind the drapes and reveal herself to his scorching gaze, he turned and walked towards the barn.

She breathed a sigh of disappointed relief and threw herself into her aunt's hammock.

It was unbearably hot. Swinging a leg over each side of the hammock, she lay back and closed her eyes, falling asleep almost instantly.

***

She sat up in bed as Frank climbed effortlessly through her bedroom window.

She should scream...but she didn't want to. After all he was only responding to the hunger he saw in her eyes every time they met his.

"I've come to fuck you," he whispered, walking over to stand at the foot of her bed. "Take off your panties and spread your legs for me."

She obeyed silently, lifting her nightgown out of the way.

He reached over, opened the lips of her vagina and rubbed his fingers along the soft inner folds before carrying them to his nose and smelling them. "Did you have a shower before you went to bed?"

"Yes."

"Good girl."

He moved back to the foot of the bed and dropped his trousers.

She watched his penis grow longer and longer, until it was as long as the stallion's had been.

"Spread your legs wider," he commanded as he took hold of his unwieldy penis and aimed it between her...

She woke to a strange, sweet sensation and opened her eyes sleepily. Rover's head was under the wide skirt of her sundress and he was enthusiastically licking the gusset of her panties.

"Rover!" She sat up and tried to push him away but he pressed his nose more insistently against her and kept licking.

Using all her strength, she tried to push the huge dog away but she couldn't budge him. Finally, she yelled, "Heel!"

Rover immediately sat back on his hunches and eyed her, his tongue hanging out of his mouth.

Her vagina felt strange. She pushed the gusset aside and found her vagina slippery and swollen.

Rover was still standing next to the hammock, panting, as if awaiting a command from her to continue what he'd been doing.

The feeling had been so delicious. She'd only stopped him because she had instinctively felt that what he'd been doing was wrong. But was it? He always licked her hands, her feet and any part of her body that was in reach, even her face if she let him. Maybe there was nothing wrong in letting him...

She jumped up as she heard the wheels of her aunt's pickup crunching the gravel on the driveway and ran to help unload the vehicle. Frank was already reaching for a sack of grain when she reached the dust-covered 4X4 Off-Roader. He slung it over one broad shoulder before reaching for another. Then he turned and headed to the barn, catching her eye and giving her a sneaky wink.

She suddenly felt weak and achy. His green eyes always seemed to see right through her and know her every desire.

"Don't just stand there, girl. Grab the groceries from the front seat," her aunt ordered, looking at her in exasperation.

Abigail snapped out of her trance and quickly moved to do as her aunt instructed.

***

"I'm going for a walk, Aunt Imelda," she informed her aunt just before dinner that evening.

"Okay but don't go too far now," her aunt warned.

"I'm just going to see the new lambs."

"Make sure you come back before it gets dark."

"Yes, Auntie."

The sun was setting as she headed across the freshly-mowed grass and she stopped to admire the startling mix of reds and oranges before moving towards the sheep pen. As she got closer she heard a strange noise coming from inside the huge structure. Cautiously, she pushed the door open and went to investigate, praying that a jaguar from the nearby forest hadn't managed to find its way inside.

She found Frank in the middle of the flock of sheep, his trousers around his ankles, his erect cock sticking out in front of him. Her knees nearly buckled at the sight of it. It was only average, surprising since he was so tall but to Abigail it looked enormous. He smiled at her, his green eyes reflecting more brown than usual as he stroked its stiffness.

"Have you ever seen a hard cock before, little girl?" he asked, his English accent seeming more pronounced.

She shook her head and he beckoned her over. She went meekly, mesmerized by the sight of his strong erection, profuse pubic hair and muscular thighs.

"Come over here and rub Uncle Frank's cock for him."

Uncle? He was almost two years younger than she was. She laughed and said, "You're not old enough to be my uncle."

"Let's pretend then."

He took her hand and led her to a corner behind several bales of hay. Placing her hands on his cock, he whispered, "Stroke it for me, little girl."

Obediently, she ran them up and down the rigid shaft.

"Have you ever been fucked?" he asked as he reached under the hem of her skirt.

She shook her head.

Pushing the crotch of her panty aside, he ran his fingers over her pussy before spanking it lightly. "Naughty girl— your pussy is wet. Did you get excited when you saw Uncle

Frank's cock?"

"Yes," she admitted.

"Would you like Uncle Frank to fuck you?"

"*Yes*," she responded eagerly. Oh yes, please! Her parents had been very protective and Aunt Imelda just as bad, but finally a chance to be fucked!

"You'll have to come back later when your aunt is sleeping," he told her. "I want to take time to savour your tight pussy but for now open your legs wider and Uncle Frank will give you a finger."

He circled her entrance with his large, coarse forefinger and slid it up inside her. She gasped at the sensation.

"Yes," Frank groaned, his strange green eyes lighting up as he pressed his calloused digit even deeper. "You're a tight little virgin."

Abigail stopped stroking his cock, lost in bliss as he started thrusting his finger back and forth.

"Keep stroking, my dear. I want to shoot my load all over your dainty hands."

She tightened her grip on him and instantly he stiffened and spurted his cum. She instinctively moved out of the way as it arched upwards.

He sat on a bale of straw, seeming oblivious to the sharp nettles of hay sticking into his bare backside as he pulled her closer by the finger in her pussy.

"Doesn't your aunt let Rover do you too?"

"Do what to me?" she asked confused.

"Never mind, Uncle Frank will do you, Rover will do her."

"Frank, I don't know what you mean."

"Don't worry your pretty head, little girl. Let Uncle Frank tongue your fat clit now."

He pulled his finger out of her and hooked her leg over his shoulder. She moaned loudly as he covered her clitoris with his mouth and sucked on it. He clasped it firmly between his lips and tugged on it until she came, her legs trembling.

She collapsed weakly against him just as her aunt called, "Abigail, dinnertime!"

"I'll see you later, my dear," he said as he quickly slid his finger back inside her now-dripping pussy up to the knuckle. "Uncle Frank will fuck this pussy *nicely* for you."

"*Abigail!*" her aunt called again.

"Coming, Aunt Imelda!" she yelled in return but opened her legs, tilting her hips up so that Frank could thrust a second finger inside her.

"You'd better go before she comes looking for you," he warned, giving her several deep, tantalizing thrusts before pulling his fingers out.

She ran back to the house, still puzzled by Frank's statement about Rover *doing* her aunt. Imelda was very possessive about the dog, she didn't even like Abigail to pet him, but what could Frank have meant?

***

Before they sat down for their meal of large pan-fried sirloin steaks her aunt took Frank's dinner out to the barn for him. Abigail still didn't understand why Frank couldn't occupy one of the spare bedrooms. When she had broached the subject her aunt had told her that it was not seemly for unmarried women to live under the same roof as a single unrelated male.

After dinner Abigail bade her aunt good night, had a shower and lay restlessly in the dark, listening as her aunt bolted windows and doors, securing the house for the night before she turned in.

As soon as the sounds coming from her aunt's bedroom ceased, Abigail slipped out of the house and headed for the barn.

Frank was waiting naked at the top of the hayloft. She swiftly climbed the ladder and joined him. His single bed was pushed against the wall but it still took up most of the limited space.

"I forgot that we'll need condoms so I'll have to make do with your tight ass tonight. Your aunt would kill me if I put a bun in your oven."

"Put a bun in my oven? What are you talking about?"

"Get you pregnant," he clarified as he pulled off her pyjama pants, turned her around and pushed her face downwards onto the narrow bed. "Lift your hips so that Uncle Frank could have a good look at you."

Obediently she pushed her ass upwards. He looked at her tightly closed asshole for a moment before wetting a finger with his saliva and pressing it against her. She moaned softly as he probed her asshole trying to gain entry. "You have a tight little asshole, Uncle Frank is going to have some trouble getting his cock inside there."

He knelt on the bed, leaned forward and rimmed her.

"No," she whispered weakly.

"Yes, my dear. Let Uncle Frank prepare your ass for his cock."

He continued for a few moments, swirling his tongue repeatedly around her anus, making her vaginal muscles clench in response and moisture drip from her entrance.

"Your pussy juices are flowing nicely," Frank remarked as he straightened. He pushed a finger into her wet vagina and then pulled it out. "I'll use some to ease the way for my cock."

He placed his juice-covered finger against her asshole and slowly forced it inside. Giving her little time to draw breath he started to thrust it in and out.

"You're a natural for ass-fucking," he commented as he added another finger as he reached upwards to roll her nipple between the thumb and forefinger of his free hand. "Your asshole's opening up beautifully already."

She moaned as he thrust them in and out of her, instinctively moving her hips in a circular motion as the pleasure intensified.

"I think that's enough for now," he told her, pulling his fingers out and placing the head of his cock against her. "I don't want to tear your asshole but I want you to feel a little pain."

"Do I really have to?" she asked as he tilted her ass upwards with his huge hands.

"Yes. The pain will ensure that you never forget that Uncle Frank was the first person to slip his cock inside your tight asshole."

"I'd never forget you," she promised.

"You will forget me as soon as your aunt finds you a suitable husband. I know she doesn't think that I'm good enough for you. She will probably find you some rich older man who will take great pleasure in fucking your asshole regularly." He pressed the head against her and warned, "Now, take a deep breath."

The lungful of air was forced out of her as he slipped the head inside her. She needed several more breaths as he pressed his cock deeper.

"Feel the sweet pain, my dear," he whispered in her ear as he kept slowly pressing inwards. "No matter who fucks your ass for the rest of your life, you'll always remember Uncle Frank's cock."

He forced more and more of his cock inwards and the barn was filled with her soft moans as her asshole stretched to accommodate his rigid cock.

"Pretend to be a little lamb, it will ease the pain."

Pretend to be a lamb?

"Go on, my dear, pretend you're a lamb for Uncle

Frank."

"You want me to bleat like a lamb?" she asked in disbelief. She'd thought he was joking when he'd said it the first time!

"Do it to please your Uncle Frank, my dear."

"Baa-aaa!"

The tentative bleat actually seemed to lessen the pain.

"Louder," Frank commanded as he withdrew almost fully and quickly drove his cock back inside her again. She couldn't help the loud bleat that escaped her. And another as he withdrew and plunged again.

"Yes, my dear, don't stop. Bleat for Uncle Frank," he instructed as he started to thrust back and forth with increasing speed, spurred on by her realistic bleats.

A few minutes later he came with a loud groan, flooding her insides with his cum. Instead of withdrawing he rolled onto his side, taking her with him. He pushed his hand under her pyjama top and moulded her breasts. And as he played with her nipples she felt him rapidly hardening again inside her. In less than two minutes he was pushing her into position in front of him and thrusting solidly into her ass again, the sound of soft bleats renting the stillness of the night. Frank took a bit longer to cum this time but within minutes he was squirting jets of sperm into her rectum.

Again he didn't withdraw; he lay back on the bed, with her on top of him facing the ceiling. "I can't get enough of your sweet ass. Are you sore, my little lamb?"

"Just a bit, Uncle Frank" she admitted as she felt him hardening inside her, again.

"That's good." He ran his hands up and down her slim body a few times before cupping her small breasts in his hands and tweaking her nipples. "Tomorrow you will think of nothing except the way I fucked you tonight."

"I'll probably be too sore to forget!" she moaned.

Frank laughed as he reached down and spanked her pussy before fingering her clitoris. "Cum for Uncle Frank before he fucks you one last time."

He caught her clitoris between thumb and forefinger and moulded it firmly.

"Aw!" The pleasure was so intense it gave a sweet pain. She backed away from his hand, pressing her ass more fully onto his rigid-again cock.

"Stop!" she begged weakly.

"No, my dear." Frank ignored her plead and continued moulding. "I want you to take my cock a bit deeper inside you."

She had thought that he had managed to get the full length inside her before but as she continued to back onto it as he teased her clit relentlessly she realized that there had been a little more of his tapering cock left outside of her.

"Yes, my dear, take all of Uncle Frank's cock into your tight asshole," Frank whispered before sticking his tongue into her ear while simultaneously slipping his finger into her vagina. Immediately she stiffened and came.

"Well done, my dear. Now make Uncle Frank cum," he ordered as he raised her hips and started to slowly thrust her ass back and forth along the length of his cock.

***

"Better go back to your bed before your aunt wakes up and finds you gone," he warned hours later as he pulled his lips off her clitoris after her third orgasm of the night.

She pulled her pyjama bottom on and he led the way down the ladder.

They stood together at the bottom just looking at each other, his 6'4" frame completely dwarfing her. Then he lifted her up into his arms and kissed her deeply before slowly lowering her feet to the ground. "The next time Uncle Frank will see to your tight pussy. I'll get the cond—"

A white shape suddenly came out from behind a bale of hay and made for Abigail. She screamed and ran behind Frank.

"It's only my Mary, she won't harm you, she's just a bit jealous."

The ewe looked anything but harmless. Frank slapped her rump and sent her back to where she'd been sleeping, then followed Abigail to the door of the barn.

"What is she doing in the barn and not with the other sheep?"

"She keeps me company," Frank explained.

"Oh." She guessed having a sheep for a pet was similar to having a dog. He must be lonely all by himself in the barn.

She slipped into the house quietly and climbed into her bed, her asshole still throbbing from the abuse Frank had subjected it to, her pussy swollen to twice its size from his spanking, tonguing and fingering. She smiled as she fell into exhausted sleep—he had fucked her *nicely* as promised.

The sounds woke her up again the next morning.

Rover panting, her aunt making strange sounds and then finally saying, "Good boy, good boy."

What was her aunt praising the dog for?

Maybe she was giving him some kind of training.

At five-forty in the morning?

She must ask Frank—if she could remember when faced with his naked body and the hunger in his green eyes.

***

Later that night she crept out again when her aunt was sleeping.

"Your aunt worked me so hard today I didn't get a chance to go and buy the condoms. So, it'll be your little ass again tonight," he told her as he stripped her naked. "Play with Uncle Frank's cock while he fingers your tight pussy to make some lubrication."

Spreading her legs, he stroked her clitoris as he dipped his head and sucked on her right nipple. She stroked his stiff cock as instructed, watching him hungrily sucking on her nipple like he was getting milk, moving his head back and forth like a lamb at its mother's teat.

Finally he lifted his head as he slid a finger into her dripping pussy.

"Was your ass nice and sore today?" he asked, his eyes sparkling at the thought.

"Yes, Uncle Frank."

"Good, I'll fuck it *nicely* again tonight. Tomorrow you will be as sore as you were today." He sat up and look down at her, his erect cock shooting up angrily from his black pubic hair. "Come, my little lamb. Turn around for Uncle Frank."

Using the juice he procured from her pussy he quickly stuck two fingers inside her rectum. Minutes later she was bleating obediently as Frank slowly buried his cock inside her again. He kept her kneeling in front of him when he came. Almost immediately he hardened again and took her a second time, fingering her clitoris until she came. He followed almost immediately.

Afterwards they lay together on the small bed, Frank's arms wrapped tightly around her to prevent her from falling off the edge.

"The ewes are coming into season and the new ram is arriving tomorrow. Come to the field when you've finished your chores and see him fuck them."

Her vagina clenched at the thought of watching the ram go around the large flock of sheep mounting ewes. "Aunt Imelda will not allow me outside."

"Don't worry, I'll tell her I need you to give me a hand with the lambs."

The next morning Abigail woke early, had her breakfast and quickly rushed to the hens' coop. She shooed the sleepy fowls into the enclosure to pick at the paddy and corn she had strewn over the ground for them. Then gathered the two and a half dozen or so eggs they had laid, mucked out their droppings and filled their feeding and water trays.

"Frank needs a hand with the lambs today," her aunt informed her when she returned to the house. Then warned, "I'll be watching the two of you."

Abigail joined Frank in the fields. Her aunt's giant new ram had been delivered when she'd been cleaning the coop. He was strutting around smelling ewes' backsides and baring his teeth appreciatively before mounting them and treating them to several quick trusts before dismounting again.

"I like to hear the little ewes bleat when it's their first time," Frank whispered as she held one of the new lambs aloft while he pretended to examine it.

"First time?" she asked puzzled.

"Some of them have come into season for the first time. You can tell by the way they bleat."

Abigail listened to the sound of the bleats and found that what Frank had said was true. The older ewes who had already had offspring barely made a sound when the big ram mated with them. The younger ewes tried to evade him and bleated loudly when he penetrated them.

"Where is Mary?" Abigail asked, looking around for the ewe.

"She's in the barn. I wouldn't let this horny ram jump on my Mary."

"Why not?" Abigail asked, puzzled. At her age, Mary should have produced two or three lambs already. "She is much older than some of the other ewes."

"She has never been mounted by any ram," Frank explained. "I couldn't bear to watch some ram push his cock into my poor Mary. I would kill him!"

"Oh!" Abigail was surprised at his vehemence. Why was he so against it?

"Listen to them carefully," Frank broke into her thoughts. "I've got the condoms. Tonight I want to hear you bleat like a little ewe when I fuck your tight pussy for the first time."

Abigail spent the rest of the day in delicious anticipation. Rover seemed able to smell her soaking wet crotch. He kept trying to get his head under her skirt. She had to keep commanding him to 'heel' softly but firmly without her aunt noticing.

She raced out of the house as soon as she heard her aunt's first snore late that evening. Her heart was beating fast by the time she got to the barn. She felt oddly more nervous than she had been the first night she had joined Frank in the hayloft.

As usual Frank was naked when she climbed up the ladder and into the loft.

"I thought you'd never get here," he said as he seized her eagerly and stripped off her nightgown. "I've been hard for hours, thinking of your tight pussy."

He pulled the blankets off the bed and spread them out onto the wooden floor, then put a condom on his stiff penis and urged her down to the floor on all-fours.

"We'll both pretend to be sheep tonight."

Frank acted the part of a horny ram to perfection— sniffing her pussy and baring his teeth in appreciation. At first, she wasn't totally acting when she played the part of the frightened ewe, his finger gave her a little pain and his cock was bigger. But after a few minutes of him sticking his nose against her asshole while he licked her clitoris made her impatient for him to mount her. He did so like a ram, climbing over her back and sliding his hard cock between her swollen pussy lips. She bleated obediently as it gradually forced its way inside her.

"Yes, my dear, bleat as Uncle Frank takes your virginity. Bleat, my dear, bleat."

***

Abigail continued to escape almost nightly to join Frank in the hayloft. Most times he would enjoy her sweet pussy but if he was out of condoms he would spend the time burying his cock in her still-tight asshole.

Early one Wednesday morning a telegram arrived for Frank. His parental grandfather was gravely ill in England and desperately wanted to see him before he died.

Imelda hurriedly booked the next available flight out on the Friday for him.

"I'll miss you," Frank whispered as he fucked Abigail *nicely* for the fourth time in a row the night before he left. "I wish you were coming with me."

"Me too," she moaned as he thrust into her swollen pussy as if he feared he would never get the chance again.

"I'll be back…as soon as… I can," he promised spurting his seed into the condom.

When he kissed her goodbye at the barn door he made her swear to keep Mary in the barn, away from the ram. She agreed and he kissed her lingeringly one last time before she raced back to the house.

The next morning she hid her tears as the taxi, taking Frank to the airport, reversed in the driveway and drove off.

He called late the next day to let them know he'd arrived safely.

***

"We have to go into town for some supplies soon," her aunt informed her as she closed the week-old newspaper and got to her feet. "I also want to see if I can get a bitch for Rover."

A bitch for Rover?

The only time Abigail had heard the word used was when her mother had fired a maid after catching her husband screwing the woman at the kitchen sink. That day they had all had lunch and then retired for siesta. Her mother had awakened from her nap to find the side of the bed where her husband usually slept empty. She had deliberately employed an older woman not wanting a young woman in the house. She had ignored crucial signs, confident that her husband wouldn't want to screw a woman almost twice his age, a woman rapidly approaching fifty and showing every one of those years on her lined face. But her husband's lacklustre performance in their bed had made the first tendrils of suspicion creep into her mind. When she had awakened that day she had known with a woman's intuition exactly what she would find her husband and the maid getting up to. She had crept silently down to the maid's room and pushed the door open, thankful that she had insisted on the bedroom door remaining unlocked at all times, using the excuse that Abigail might wake up frightened and come to the maid's room for comfort. The truth was that she had wanted to be able to check the woman's room routinely for signs of sexual intercourse. She also knew if the door was locked, her husband could make his escape through the bedroom window before the maid let her into the room.

The maid's bed had been neatly made as usual and Abigail's mother had sighed in relief as she made her way up to the upper storey to their extensive library. Halfway up the stairs she had turned to get herself a glass of water.

She'd entered the kitchen to find the old maid bent over a sink of soapy dishes and her husband's cock buried inside the woman's grey-haired pussy. She had screamed and pulled him off before dragging the woman to her room to pack her few belongings.

Abigail had awakened to the sound of her mother screaming abuse at the woman, the words 'fucking bitch' peppering each sentence. Her father had tried to calm his irate wife but she hadn't stopped until the woman had disappeared from sight around the bend in the path.

***

"Wake up, bitch," her aunt yelled as she shook her awake. "Rover wants to fuck you."

Abigail opened her eyes and sat up.

Her aunt was standing at the side of her bed with a panting Rover beside her.

"But, Auntie, he's a dog and I'm a girl."

"That doesn't matter—he's been fucking me for years," her aunt said as she climbed on to the bed and pulled Abigail back against her. Abigail tried to struggle but her aunt held her immobile without effort, pulling her nightshirt off as she ordered, "Take off her panties, Rover."

The dog grabbed the side of Abigail's panties between his jaws and pulled them down her legs.

"Lick her until she is nice and wet, Rover," her aunt commanded. "She's a virgin and your cock is very meaty."

Rover started to lave Abigail's pussy, his rough tongue making her juices flow copiously. She tried to close her legs but she seemed to lack the strength. He licked her to two mammoth orgasms and then sat back on his heels and said, "This bitch is no virgin, Imelda.

"Of course she is," Imelda insisted.

Rover sniffed Abigail's pussy and shook his head in disagreement, "I know a virgin pussy when I smell one and this one smells like it's been fucked before."

"Impossible!" Imelda roared. "I have been watching her closely. She hasn't had the opportunity to lose her virginity!"

"If you don't believe me, stick your finger inside her and see."

Imelda pulled Abigail's legs upwards as she threatened, "If you've let that common young man fuck you I will be furious."

Abigail felt her aunt's finger...

She woke with a start her heart racing.

Her aunt hadn't wanted the responsibility of having a young woman under her roof. Her first thought after the funerals of her only sister and her brother-in-law had been to send their daughter, Abigail, to live in a convent. It had taken a lot of her niece's tears for her to finally relent. Abigail knew if her aunt ever found out she was sleeping with Frank, she would probably fire him or send *her* to live in the convent.

She snuggled her face into the pillows and closed her eyes, thankful that it was only another dream.

But what did Aunt Imelda do for sex? she thought sleepily.

She had once heard a hired farmhand refer to her aunt as a roving 'dyke' but she was sure her aunt wasn't a lesbian. She'd never remembered to ask Frank what he had meant when he'd said about Rover 'doing' her aunt.

Fragments of the conversation she'd had with Imelda in her dream came floating back to her.

Seconds later she bolted upright again as something clicked.

No, not her Aunt Imelda and Rover!

It wasn't possible! Yet, as she replayed the sounds that awakened her every morning, a sick realization filled her. And her aunt was *too* possessive with Rover. Few people would object to another person petting their dog but Aunt Imelda always called Rover to 'heel' whenever he sniffed around Abigail.

There was definitely more between her aunt and the dog than met the eye.

Abigail watched them closely in the days following. Her aunt was always stroking the dog's head and the tip of its fat pink penis was constantly jutting out.

The early morning sounds continued unabated until

Abigail couldn't take it any longer. Filled with curiosity and dread, she slipped out of the house one morning as soon as the sounds began. Placing a ladder noiselessly against the side of the house, she climbed up and peered into her aunt's bedroom window.

They were at it!

Abigail stared at them in shock.

Her aunt was covered in sweat and so was Rover. His beautiful glossy black coat shone wetly as he ran on his canine treadmill which was placed beside her aunt's state-of-the-art, larger, wider one.

Laughter threatened Abigail as she descended the ladder. Returning it to the tool shed, she raced back up to her bedroom and buried her face into a pillow to stifle her laughter as she listened to her aunt and Rover finish their morning exercise.

***

The next day Imelda and Abigail drove to Rio de Janeiro.

"I am hoping the bitch this man has for sale is suitable for Rover," her aunt said as she parked in front of a small freshly-painted house. "Stay in the vehicle, I won't be too long."

Abigail's heart started beating faster. She had completely forgotten her aunt's promise to get a bitch for Rover. She waited with morbid fascination to see the woman who would let Rover mount her.

Five minutes later her aunt came from behind the building with a large dog on a leash.

Weak with relief, she remembered that the term meant female dog.

"Her name is Betsy," Imelda introduced the very friendly dog to Abigail before opening the back door for the dog to scramble up into the vehicle. "I hope Rover will like her."

"I'm sure he will, Auntie." Abigail reached behind and

patted the dog again. "She is lovely."

"It's not as simple as that. I rescued Rover from the dog sanctuary. They were going to put him down because he was considered an unsuitable pet." Imelda paused briefly, took a deep breath and continued, "I think his previous owners made him perform unspeakable acts."

"Why do you think that, Auntie?"

"When I first got him, I left him in the kennel outside and he howled until I couldn't stand it and brought him into the house. He immediately jumped up on my bed. I ordered him off and he curled up on the mat next to it. The next morning as soon as I got off the bed he started to hump my leg. I managed to break him of the habit but he still tries to sniff under my clothes. I have to constantly tell him to 'heel'. That's why I keep him away from you."

"But that doesn't mean that his previous owner let him to nasty things," Abigail protested.

"Darling, you're young and you've lived a very sheltered life but believe me some people do terrible things with animals. The old man who owned the farm next to mine was definitely a sheep-shagger."

"Sheep-shagger? What's that?"

"Yes. He was caught on numerous occasions doing nasty things to his ewes. I wouldn't be surprised if he died from some terrible disease he contracted from one of them."

"Is that why the farm is abandoned?"

"His wife caught him with one of the ewes, so she took the children and went back to São Paulo. He died a lonely, old man."

"That's so sad."

"He got what he deserved—he had *no* right to shag an animal."

***

"I'll chain her to the kennel for a few days to make sure

she doesn't escape. I paid twice what I had planned for her but she is pure breed like Rover, their puppies will be worth a lot of money if I decide to sell them," Imelda explained as she secured Betsy's chain to the post near the kennel which Rover had refused to sleep in. "The vet said she was in her first heat—that should make her more susceptible to Rover's advances."

Rover came racing out of the house excitedly and greeted his new friend, licking her face before swiftly moving to her rump to investigate the streaming nub under her tail. He licked it enthusiastically, the head of his pink penis jutting out of its penile covering.

"Keep an eye on them while I put the groceries away." Imelda picked up her carrier bags and walked towards the house, leaving Abigail to watch avidly as Rover mounted Betsy and housed his penis inside her with several vigorous canine thrusts before he scrambled off her back, bringing his forelegs back on to the ground.

Abigail was amazed to see that although he now faced away from Betsy, he was still attached to her. She had only ever seen the tip of his penis and was even more amazed at the thickness of the shaft embedded in the now-whimpering Betsy. Abigail wondered if it hurt Betsy as much to lose her virginity as it had hurt her when Frank had taken hers.

"Don't worry, Betsy, the first time is the worst," she whispered consolingly to the dog. "You will like it better the second time."

"Come away and leave them now, Abigail," her aunt shouted from the front door. "I just wanted to ensure that they wouldn't fight each other."

Abigail gave the mating dogs one last look and reluctantly headed for the house.

The table was already laid for dinner. Abigail carried the heavy casserole dish to the dining room before returning for the crisp green salad while her aunt sliced freshly-baked, crusty homemade bread.

They ate the meal in relative silence. Her aunt enjoying the treat of reading the same day's newspapers, while Abigail's thoughts were filled with images of Rover and Betsy. The dog didn't appear at the table to beg for titbits as he usually did during the meal; he obviously found mounting Betsy more satisfying than the scraps Abigail discreetly fed him whenever her aunt had her head buried in a newspaper.

As soon as the meal ended, Abigail washed the dishes. She kissed her aunt goodnight and hurried to her bedroom eagerly. She had remembered during the meal that the kennel was just below her window, she would have an unobstructed view of Rover and Betsy.

She was just in time to see Rover mounting Betsy again. Minutes later they were stuck together, again.

Rover was insatiable, it seemed that every time Abigail checked he was either licking Betsy, mounting her or facing away from her, his penis stuck deep inside her. Every time Abigail saw them mating her vagina ached in hunger and she missed Frank even more.

Finally three and a half months after he'd left, Frank called to say that his grandfather had died. He was making arrangements for the funeral and would be back by the next week. He was his grandfather's sole heir and there were a few legalities that had to be observed before he returned to Brazil.

***

Abigail jumped out of bed as soon as Aunt Imelda's first snore rent the air. She ran to the barn her heart light. As she opened the door she heard bleating and the grunting sounds Frank made when he was making love to her.

She heard him say, "Yes, Mary, my dear, bleat for Uncle Frank."

The bleating reached a crescendo as Frank's grunts grew louder....

Abigail woke up with a scream.

Not Frank!

He couldn't be a sheep-shagger! He couldn't!

Had he been merely masturbating the day she caught him among the sheep? Or had he been about to fuck one of the ewes?

Why was Mary really sleeping in the barn? And why was she so possessive when it came to Frank? Why hadn't Frank wanted the new ram to mount her? Was it because he was mounting her himself?

And why did Frank insist on Abigail bleating every time he fucked her?

Oh God! He *was* a sheep-shagger!

***

Frank arrived by taxi late Thursday evening. Abigail stood by her aunt's side and watched him pay the driver after retrieving his two heavy suitcases from the booth of the car. He was almost unrecognizable; he looked absolutely nothing like the young man who had left less than four months ago. He was clean-shaven, had cut off his long ponytail, was wearing designer jeans and a polo shirt and looked incredibly handsome.

"Hello, Miss Imelda. Hi, Abigail." His British accent was even more pronounced and it sent a delicious shiver down Abigail's spine as she responded to his greeting.

"Hello, Frank," Imelda replied, surprising them both when she invited, "Come on inside, you must be exhausted. I have made one of the spare bedrooms ready for you."

Both Frank and Abigail stood looking at her.

"I had planned to…to go over to the farm later today," Frank said, clearly thrown by Imelda's unexpected invitation.

"It won't be fit for you to live in for another couple of days," Imelda explained. "I had it thoroughly cleaned and arranged for it to be painted tomorrow. It will need airing for at least a day before you can move in."

Abigail had heard her aunt on the phone earlier in the week issuing instructions for what sounded like a massive cleanup operation but she'd had no idea that she'd been doing so on Frank's behalf.

"You bought the farm next door?" she asked Frank in surprise as her aunt lifted one of the suitcases and turned to go indoors.

"Yes," he confirmed, grabbing the handle of the other suitcase and gesturing for her to precede him.

Imelda had held dinner, waiting for his arrival. They sat down and ate immediately. Abigail couldn't keep her eyes off him, he was so familiar and yet like a stranger. She glanced at his hands as he expertly wielded her aunt's best silver. Those fingers had been up inside her, arousing her, stretching her so that he could slip inside her. She looked up and caught his green eyes on her breasts. They darkened as her nipples hardened involuntarily under the thin cotton of her dress. He looked up and their eyes caught and held.

"What's going on here?" Imelda's voice startled them both. "Have you been sleeping with my niece?"

"Miss Imelda…" Frank's voice trailed off as Abigail shook her head in warning.

Instead of seeming upset, her aunt was smiling as she poured after-dinner brandies into small tumblers before continuing, "I hope you plan to make an honest woman of her."

"I intend to marry her if she will have me."

Did she want to marry a sheep-shagger?

"Of course, she will have you!" Imelda replied, giving her niece no choice.

***

Imelda was excited at the prospect of having her niece marry a millionaire. She swiftly made all the arrangements for a quiet wedding a week later. As she had predicted the house was habitable two days later and Frank had moved in, taking Mary with him.

I should have let the ram mount her, Abigail thought jealously as she watched Frank slowly drive away the brand-new Range Rover that had been delivered for him the day before, Mary on the front passenger seat which was still covered in protective film.

That night she tossed and turned, her mind conjuring images of him and Mary that invaded her sleep when she finally dropped off.

She didn't see him again until their wedding day.

After the brief ceremony, Imelda insisted on sharing a meal with them before they drove over to Frank's new residence. Over the meal he discussed his plans for his stud farm. He had already used a part of his substantial inheritance to purchase six thoroughbred mares and a magnificent stallion. Abigail almost came sitting at the dining table at the thought of watching the stallion and the mares mate.

Frank's new house was larger than her aunt's. He gallantly lifted her from the vehicle, took her over the threshold and straight up to the master bedroom. He stripped off her simple wedding dress and laid her onto the bed before getting undressed himself. When he joined her on the bed, he took her in his arms and just held her, much to her surprise.

"I want to talk to you before we make love."

Make love? What about fucking?

"Okay," she agreed, hoping that the change in his appearance didn't indicate a change in the way he fucked.

"I found my mother's diary...I know why she shot my father."

Abigail waited patiently for him to continue. He didn't.

Finally she urged, "Go on."

"She found out that he had regularly cheated on her with a prostitute."

"A prostitute?" Abigail asked, shocked.

"When I was about ten years old he started taking me to football practice on Monday and Wednesday," Frank continued without answering her question. "On Friday he would make my mother dress me as though I was going to practice but instead we went to visit a young woman called Violet. The two of them would go into the bedroom and leave me to watch cartoons on her TV but I was still able to hear sounds coming from her bedroom. I had no idea what they were doing until I peeped through the keyhole when I was about thirteen. He bent her over a chair and said, 'Bleat like a little lamb while Uncle Sam fucks you, my dear.' On the way home I told him that I'd peeped through the keyhole. He told me that he didn't mind me watching but made me promise that I wouldn't tell my mother. By the time I was fourteen he was letting me have a go after he had finished. He made her call me 'Uncle Frank' and bleat as I fucked her. I don't know how my mother found out but in her diary she wrote that she was devastated that he had corrupted me as well."

"I'm so sorry," Abigail consoled.

"I wonder if he was a sheep-shagger?" Frank said the words almost to himself as he ran his hand up her flat stomach and cupped her breast.

"Are you?" she asked quickly, glad that he had brought the subject up.

"Am I what?"

"A sheep-shagger?"

"Of course not! Why would you ask such a question?"

"What about Mary?"

"What about her?"

"Did you ever *shag* her?"

"Never!" Frank denied, astonishment written all over his face. "When my grandfather sent me back here, I had no one to talk to. Her mother had just died and she seemed as lonely as I was, so I used to curl up with her in the hay at night."

"So what were you doing the day I saw you in the sheep pen?"

"I was pleasuring myself," Frank admitted, a faint blush colouring his cheekbones. "Imagining you bleating as I fucked you."

"Oh," she sighed in relief.

"Before I went away I didn't know any better and I made you do things that I shouldn't have," Frank apologized, slipping a finger inside her slick pussy. "From now on I won't disrespect you by having anal sex wit you again, making you call me 'Uncle Frank' or bleating like a lamb."

Never fuck my ass again? Never call you Uncle Frank again? And never bleat again? Abigail thought in dismay. *But I enjoyed those things!*

"Unless you want to," her new husband continued. "I will not force you to do anything you are not comfortable with."

"I will call you 'Frank' and stop bleating but maybe for now we should continue to have anal sex," Abigail conceded. "We shouldn't make too many changes all at once."

"You're right," Frank agreed as he moistened another finger and probed her asshole. "I would miss fucking this sweet asshole."

"Not as much as it would miss *you* fucking it." She turned to get onto all-fours.

"Not doggy-style," he said as he hooked her legs over his massive shoulders and placed the head of his cock against her pussy. "We are not animals."

She gasped as he slowly pushed inside her, feeling the need to bleat to ease the pain as his cock re-acquainted itself with the tightness of her pussy.

Maybe if she did it silently.

Baa-aaa!

That's better. Maybe just another little one.

Baa-aaa!

***

The Rover and Betsy romance is inspired by real events. As a young girl in Guyana I was awakened from sleep one night by the racket of howling dogs. I peeped through the window and saw at least a dozen dogs outside our cast-iron front gate all trying to find a way into our yard. The country, like neighbouring Brazil, is very hot so pets are usually kept outside. Our little bitch, who was in her first heat, was chained to her kennel just inside the gate but her leash was long enough for her to rub noses with the other dogs through the metalwork or turn around occasionally so they could lick her. The little hussy!

Suddenly one of the biggest dogs I have ever seen strolled up and joined the others. He was an unusual shade: brown with black stripes—as if a tiger had mated with his mother. He too started sniffing our bitch and getting excited. Then, to my surprise, he took a few paces backwards, raced up to our high fence and cleared it with a single jump. Our bitch greeted him enthusiastically but I was a little concerned in case he started fighting with her; he was more than twice her size. But he soon relieved my worries as he started to lick her, showing no aggression whatsoever. He didn't have to jump up onto our bitch's back, she was so short she fit under him. I swear he had to bend his knees to get inside her. I don't think our bitch had had any idea what he had in store for her when she'd greeted him with such eagerness but as soon as he started to mate with her she started yelping and trying to bite him. He gave her a few warning growls that kept her quiet as he continued his fast doggy thrusts. When his penis was firmly embedded he moved off her back. They strained away from each other held by the knot in his penis, looking absurd because even though he was making an effort to stoop, her hind legs were literally raised off the ground.

I watched them until they finally parted a good fifteen minutes to half an hour later. And every night after that. Until my mother wised up to his visits and locked our bitch away at night. Months later she had a litter of puppies that all had patches of brown with black stripes, one even looked exactly like him. The randy devil!

*****

SUGAR BROWN

*H*ey, boys! Are those erections? I guess you are happy to see me. I'm pleased to see you too but let me warn you— I'll fuck you only once before I move on.

Lexy says I give women a bad name. I don't know why. I'm a serial fucker *not* a serial killer! Personally, I think she's jealous. Bitches never like me but I don't care because I don't like them either. I'm not fucking *no* woman so if you are looking for some lesbian action you won't find it here— close the book you're done reading.

But where are my manners? Let me introduce myself before we go any further. My name is Sugar. I was born in Guyana, in a county called Demerara so I am the real article—Demerara Sugar—not some tasteless sweetener or sugar substitute. I'm so sweet I rot teeth!

My parents moved to the UK when I was four years old. My sister Nectar was born within a year and three years later my mother had Honey Comb.   I know what you are thinking, *why all the fucking syrupy names?* Well, my mother's name is Sweetie…you guess the rest.

Having a name like Sugar is not without its problems— men want to taste me all the time, which is fine but one taste and they are hooked. The first man I fucked stalked me for months afterwards.

I met him at Corks Wine Bar Nightclub a month before my nineteenth birthday. From the moment I walked into the club my eyes connected with his. He walked over, introduced himself and we started dancing. He was about 6'3" and even though I was wearing high heels he towered over me, but he adjusted himself to my height and we danced through the 'erection section'. The brother had hands like an octopus—I swear they were on several parts of my body at the same time.

My mother had warned us about sleeping with men on the first date, which by the way I've been doing for years and *not* a damn thing has happened to me, so when we left the nightclub I gave him my number which he saved under the name 'Pure Honey'. When we got to Trafalgar Square I missed the N25 heading in my direction. While we were waiting for the next bus he managed to convince me to come to his place by giving me a sneaky finger-fuck although the Square was teeming with people. But most of them were drunk, or like us, too busy getting it on to notice.

I decided then to sleep with him. I had been masturbating from a tender age and hadn't really felt the need for real sex but it wasn't like I'd been saving myself for marriage. So we jumped on the N159 and made our way to Brixton. He still lived at home with his parents but they were visiting his father's brother in California. His two younger sisters were in bed when we got there. He was an untidy fucker—we had to use his parents' bed because his bedroom was a mess. When he pushed his bedroom door open I told him plain, *"Hell, fucking no!"* It was *Jumanji* in there. All kinds of wild animals must have taken sanctuary in that undisturbed refuge. Hell, a snake could have crawled up into my pussy and fucked me if I had fallen asleep on his bed without my drawers on.

He licked me from head to toe, sucking on my nipples and clit until I was moaning so loudly he had to cover my mouth so I didn't wake his sisters. He had a nice cock: tapering from a small head to a thick base. While we were fucking he kept saying, "Shit, you're as tight as a virgin!" His face when he was cumming put me off slightly—his eyes bulged and he literally foamed at the mouth—not a pretty sight! He didn't hurt me much and I was quite surprised that I bled at all. When he pulled his cock out of me and saw a bit of blood, he was shocked. "Why the hell didn't you tell me you were a fucking virgin?" he demanded. Why should I have told him? He would have still fucked me, wouldn't he? He went ape-shit—all kindness and consideration because he was the first. Don't ask me why. It wasn't as if he had just won a race and was going to get a medal or a prize. He insisted on giving me a lift home but needed to snooze off some of the alcohol he had consumed before he drove.

He held onto me so tightly while he slept I couldn't have escaped if I wanted to. I wasn't used to that kind of sweaty body contact so I didn't sleep a wink. When he woke up I pulled myself away and by chance looked down at his cock. It had retreated back into itself, looking small and defenceless, like a little boy's. I knew that it could get erect again but the thought of him sticking it back into me didn't appeal to me. I developed an instant phobia for sleeping with the same man *twice*.

I didn't want to fuck him again but he kept pestering me. Telling me that he was special—my first man and it should mean something to me. But I honestly couldn't see what difference it made first or fifty-first!

He called my mobile phone so often I regretted giving him my number. He wouldn't leave me alone so I took a day off work, put on an old school uniform and went to his office two corners from St Paul's Station, taking Honey

Comb's birth certificate with me. He always called me 'Honey' although I had told him my name when he'd introduced himself. I could have taken Nectar's but she was fifteen and I didn't want him to start bothering me again when I *supposedly* reached the age of consent the following year.

I felt terrible as I watched him rush from his desk to throw up his breakfast when he thought that he'd messed with a twelve-year-old. But *really*, he was an up-and-coming criminal lawyer and should have known better; he hadn't even asked me how old I was before we had fucked. I always have to produce ID because I'm petite. My sisters used to laugh their heads off when I took them to a club or bar when they were underaged, and they were allowed inside but I had to take out my driver's licence to prove my age.

He never called me again but they say a girl always remembers her first lover. I do. His name was Wendell Skeete. I remember him more for the way he stalked me than the way he fucked me.

I learned my lesson with him. No exchange of telephone numbers or names—just fuck and split. Guys tell me that I operate 'like a man' losing interest once I've had them. I tell them I operate like me—I don't see *them* ready to move on after one fuck.

You name them, I've slept with them: teachers, bouncers, waiters, barmen, scuba divers, gymnasts, athletes, government ministers, pilots, doctors, lawyers, footballers, male nurses, garbage men, musicians, DJs, the unemployed...even a pastor and a bridegroom on his wedding night...I don't discriminate. As far as I'm concerned only one cock is off-limits and that's my father's—my mother would bitch-slap me if I messed with her cock, *and* he's over forty. I won't fuck a man over forty because I like a man to be able to get his cock hard again as soon as he cums because I don't have the time or the patience to wait until he has a rest before we can fuck again. I won't sleep with a boy under sixteen either because I don't want to end up in jail for some underdeveloped cock.

I don't have female friends. Women get edgy when I am around their men, and I don't know why. All I will do is fuck them once and give them back. What's wrong with borrowing another woman's cock one time? It's the women who want a relationship with their men that these women have to worry about, not me.

***

I never understand why a guy asks a woman to say his name when he's fucking her. At best she will think he's dumb—old enough to fuck but too dense to remember his own name. Or worst case scenario, a woman he really loves will call him by another man's name and then he's totally fucked. If a man asks me what's his name while he is fucking me I tell him straight, 'I don't fucking know'. It's usually true—how the hell am I expected to remember a guy's name when we'd only met for the first time the very day? The only guys' names I remember are the ones who played hard-to-get and made me go chasing after them. You know, the ones who don't believe in one-night stands and won't fuck on a first date. They bring out the hunter in me. I pretend to be interested in a long-term relationship and let them wine and dine me. As soon as I fuck them, I drop them.

Cock size doesn't matter to me—once it's big I'm okay. Now, don't get an attitude you small-cock brother, I am doing you a favour, baby—my pussy will eat up and spit out a cock of less than six *fat* inches. And no, my pussy isn't slack, it's your cock that's small!

Did I say women don't like me? Men don't like me much either. Okay, they like me before we fuck but once they realize that I'm not going to fuck them again they get pissed off and start calling me names like 'whore' and 'slut'. Like I give a damn! I would change my name to Slut Brown if I could find the time between fucks to get up to the registry, deed-poll office or wherever it is one goes to get one's fucking name changed. I'm thinking of approaching the *Guinness Book of World Records* because surely I must hold the record in the category: Highest Number of Black Men Fucked by Single Black Female. I'm very proud of my sexual achievements and would like the recognition due to me. And why shouldn't I be proud? I'm a die-hard feminist and believe in equality in all aspects of life. When guys fuck anything that moves, people call them *sweet-men* but they are basically *man-whores* or *man-sluts*. So, if they can be proud of their-fucking-selves why can't I?

See, you're starting to hate me already and we probably haven't fucked yet. I say probably because there is a good chance if you are a young, big-cocked, Black male from Guyana, London or St Lucia that I have fucked you.

By the way, did you know the way a man fucks is dependant on where he was born? True! British guys are pretty good in bed, they will tongue your pussy and fuck you nicely. Guyanese men are excellent fuckmen but most of them will not eat a pussy. This may soon change because I am single-handedly working to bring them into the pussy-eating 21st century. St Lucian men know how to suck a pussy and they have some of the biggest cocks in the world. Hail up, my St Lucian brothers—you pussy-eating, big-cock swinging, fucking connoisseurs!

Okay, maybe I'm a bit biased at the moment because finally a man has me sprung and he happens to be St Lucian.

But I'm getting ahead of myself.

Rewind.

***

My sister Nectar told you about me in *Bedtime Erotica for Freaks (like me)* so I won't bore you with the details. The only thing I like more than fucking is designing websites. I have thousands of clients but I work freelance, so I came to St Lucia a few years ago to sample some of the prime cock I had heard about. I can't remember the exact date I arrived but I can tell you about the man who fucked me the very night. I keep track of cocks *not* time, it is easier for me. Let me see, I've had one cock per week, although I've occasionally had two, so I've been here about...one hundred and thirty-seven cocks since arrival divided by fifty-two...just over two and a half years. Sounds about right.

Every three months *or* after cock number thirteen, I go for a dip in the Island's beautiful Sulphur Springs. I am not superstitious but it feels right to purge after thirteen men in a row. After the dip I feel rejuvenated and so does my pussy.

Three weeks ago I met Berry for the first time. His name is Renee but women call him Blackberry because he's Black and sweet. I call him Berry because saying, 'fuck me, Blackberry' doesn't have the same ring to it as 'fuck me, Berry'. I can be a bit loud when a man is fucking me, I don't want anyone overhearing and thinking that I'm fucking a fruit.

I told him plain when I met him that I don't fuck the same man twice. He told me that wasn't a problem because he has women queuing for him and once he'd fucked me I would have to get on the back of the queue if I wanted to be fucked again. Talk about having a monumental ego! He pissed me the hell off! But I didn't say anything because I knew once he had a taste of my 'sugar' he would instantly develop a sweet tooth. He is 5'10", broad-shouldered and slim-waisted with skin so dark and smooth you want to bite it. But his dark grey eyes are what make women go weak at the knees. The contrast of his eyes against his dark skin is so amazing you can help but stare when you meet him.

I never paid attention to a man's eyes before I met Berry. They weren't that important to me—I have fucked two blind men; as I said before, I don't discriminate. And I treated them no differently from other men—I fucked them both *once* before I moved on just like I usually do. Just like I did the Paralympic gold medallist I'd met at a black-tie dinner and dance at a posh hotel. He had lost the use of his legs in a car accident and had extremely powerful arms. I had gone to the dinner as a footballer's date but one look at the wheelchair-bound man's huge arms and I had to fuck him. He must have sensed it because he winked at me before leaving his table and heading for the washroom. We quickly slipped inside the disabled toilet without being seen. I don't usually fuck in toilets but the hotel's were roomy and spotless. We used his wheelchair. After he had bent me over his knees, he fingered my asshole and then instructed me to back it onto him. He then grabbed me by the waist and plonked me on top of his big cock without ceremony. I didn't have to do a thing for almost five minutes, as he lifted me up and down on. When I sensed that he was tiring I grabbed the arms of the wheelchair and rode him like he was a stallion. Of course he wanted my details afterwards but I just smiled sweetly as I wiped myself off and then walked out. The fool didn't wait a couple of minutes to avoid suspicion. He put his cock away and caught up with me before I got back to my table.

The footballer eyed us suspiciously and wanted to know where I had gotten to. I whispered discreetly that I'd had a slight anal problem, but I was fine now. It's best to tell the truth—no one believes it.

He had booked us a room at the same hotel for the night. A soon as we entered it he whipped out his flaccid cock and told me to get down on my knees and suck it. Tall, arrogant, young fucker like him and his cock hadn't even stirred at the prospect of fucking me. And it was small. I told him that I had fucked the wheelchair guy who had a cock twice the size of his and left. He is a multimillionaire now, one of Chelsea's star footballers but whenever I see him in the papers all I see is his small, limp cock hanging out of his black Armani trousers.

But back to Berry. Isn't it strange for a man to be called Renee? He is man enough to carry the *girly* name but I prefer to call him Berry because worse than people thinking that I am fucking fruit would be for them to think that I am fucking another woman. Don't get me wrong, I don't have a problem with lesbians—I often masturbate watching girl-on-girl porn but I will not sleep with another woman. I love cocks far too much and no! a fake cock won't do! Once I met a bitch in a party. She had her hair cropped like a man, had dressed like a man, and had danced with me and kissed me all night like she was a fucking man. She had even put something in her trousers for me to rub up against. Bitch! She had strapped her breasts down and though her chest had felt a little bit strange at first, the hard *cock* soon distracted me. When the party was over she followed me to my car like a fucking gentleman. It was just after five in the morning but bright enough for me to see her face clearly. Man, I cursed her in fine fucking style. I had set myself up for a good round of cock to round up the evening and she couldn't even fucking deliver! The bitch then had the nerve to tell me not to knock it before I tried it. Lucky I didn't *knock* her out.

***

Berry invited me to his place after we met at the Sulphur Springs.

He has a small, neat house close to the beach with every kind of fruit tree imaginable in his backyard. He is a joiner by trade and had made almost everything in his house, including the bed he tossed me onto as soon as we got indoors.

"Right, English girl, let's see if you can handle this St Lucian cock."

He was naked in seconds and I stared in amazement at his big cock. Most cocks have a slight left or right hook; his veered not once but twice—it was zigzag and I found it strangely beautiful.

"Fuck! How long is that cock?" I asked.

"Eleven…eleven and a quarter, depending on the weather," he replied casually as if having a cock almost as long as a ruler was nothing unusual.

"Fuck!" It was the only word I could think of as my brain refused to function.

It wasn't the size of his cock that bothered me, it was the run of bad luck I'd had recently. Most of the guys I had slept with in the last three months had been *small* large, the minimum cock size I work with. A few of them had been what I considered *medium* large. Berry was a *ex-large* large and it was quite a jump from the last man to him. Plus I swear the Sulphur Springs makes my pussy tighter.

"I hope you are not about to back down after all the talk you were giving me in the car."

"Hell, no!" I would rather end up in hospital than back down from his cock! But shit where did a man his height get a cock that size from?

"I like a nice, wet pussy."

Before I could start undressing, he pushed my skirt up and ripped my thong off me.

"Hey!"

"You'll be too sore to wear it later," he informed me and spread my pussy lips. "Hold on to something or you will end up on the floor."

"What the hell are you talking ab—? Fuck!"

I quickly grabbed the headboard as a sharp, sweet sensation ran from my pussy straight to my brain and exploded. Dazed, I raised my head to see what he was doing. His tongue was moving like lightning, flicking and swirling around my clit so fast the pleasure came in one huge wave. I felt the hairs on my body raise simultaneously just as I clamped his head between my thighs and came harder than I had ever done in my life!

He pressed my legs apart and quickly thrust two fingers inside me while I was still cumming and it instantly sent me into another orgasm. I had to bite my lip to stop screaming out loud.

He rolled me over to reach for the short zip on my skirt and I went with the movement, as limp as a rag doll. I let him undress me, needing a few minutes to catch my equilibrium but trying not to show it. When he spread my legs and started to lower himself between them I snapped out of my trance.

I quickly sat up, pushed him back against the bed and wrapped my lips around the head of his cock. I knew I was in trouble as soon as it hit the back of my throat while there was still enough left outside for me to wrap both hands around. But trouble aside, it was the sweetest cock I've ever tasted and I have tasted a few, give or take a thousand. His pre-cum was delish! It must have been something to do with what he puts into his body. He drinks water by the litre and eats lots of fresh, organic, home-grown fruit and vegetables. Most days he catches a fish or two, some crayfish or a lobster for lunch after his morning swim.

He moved his hips to match my rhythm as I gave him head. Suddenly he stiffened and filled my mouth with the most delicious cum I have ever tasted. I swallowed every drop, even licking up a drop that had dared to escape my lips and fall onto his lower belly. I covered the head of his cock again to make sure that I had gotten every last millilitre and felt it harden. So, I continued, hoping for another serving of his thick cum but at the last minute he sat up and wrestled his cock away from me.

"I'm ready for some pussy now."

Trouble!

His cock is not bulbous but it's the same *thick* girth from tip to base. I don't admit to crying but my eyes watered a bit as he tried to get the head inside me.

"I thought you told me in the car that your pussy expands to fit *any* size of cock," Berry complained as he pulled back and tried an extra finger.

"I meant any *normal* sized cock—your cock is XXXL!"

"I don't usually have this much trouble getting into a pussy!"

What did he usually fuck? Mares? Cows?

"Ah!" He sounded so victorious as his cock slipped inside me you'd think he'd just re-discovered the atom.

I like to look at myself being fucked—it turns me on, so I glanced down. My pussy lips were stretched so wide I wondered abstractly if they would regain their former shape but I didn't let it worry me too much as I watched him slowly fill my pussy. Things went smoothly until he got to the first bend in his cock. But he must have encountered the same problem before because he simply lifted my hips and turned me from side to side, like he was a screwdriver and his cock, a screw he was trying to get into me. He got stuck at the second bend but again he quickly navigated around it and finally I was filled with more cock than I have ever had in my life.

"This is some good pussy, English girl," he said, as he lowered himself on top of me.

"I know, baby."

He lay still for a moment, I suspect to let my pussy adjust

itself to his cock, and then started to slowly move his hips. When he pulled back a couple of inches and slid his cock back inside me the two bends touched nerve endings in my pussy that I had been unaware I possessed.

Fuck!

"You like this cock, English girl?"

Like his cock? I fucking loved it!

"It's alright," I replied.

"Alright...?"

I waited for him to continue but he didn't. Instead he withdrew almost the entire length of his cock and gave it back to me in a quick thrust. I shot up the bed but the headboard stopped me from going too far. He pulled me back under him and continued to pummel my pussy with deep, hard, fast strokes.

"Your cock's the best, baby," I admitted as I grabbed a handful of his dreadlocks and pulled his lips down to mine.

I don't like to give too much praise in case men get cocky but sometimes you have to admit the truth.

***

I was sore for days.

And the thing is...I haven't looked at another man since and it's been over three weeks. I can't keep this shit up or it will throw off my calendar—how am I going to know what week of the year it is if I don't keep fucking at least one guy weekly?

I broke my rule and gave him my number, now he keeps calling me. He wants to fuck me again. He told me that his cock gets hard whenever he thinks of the head I gave him and he's been thinking about my pussy night and day. But is that a good enough reason to give it to him again? His cock looks good when it is not erect so I don't have to worry about that particular phobia but I can't imagine what it will be like fucking the same guy *twice*.

I was so confused I wrote to Nectar last week begging her for some advice. I wanted to know what love felt like because I am getting the urge to fuck Berry again and I have never felt that urge before. Is it love or just the fact that he has the biggest cock that I have ever come across? She is the only sister who has had the experience of having regular boyfriends. She is very happy at the moment with her men Tom and Jerry and their little daughter, Sherry.

Honey Comb, doesn't share my phobia but like me she will generally only sleep with a man once, unless he is very good in bed. But even if he is a great lay she will kick him to the curb within a week or two when she gets bored. Terry is the only man she's ever let fuck her regularly and I guess it's because he is well-behaved. He goes over to her flat to fuck her whenever she calls him and leaves when she wants him to. He wants to marry her and at first she had said no. She never wanted children but she loves Sherry so much she is thinking of having a child of her own. And she has nothing to lose, Terry says that he doesn't mind if she sleeps with other men after they are married.

Berry is probably the one for me. Maybe we will settle down, have little *sugarberries* and live happily ever after.

So hail up the thousands of men I've fucked! Commiserations to the unlucky ones I haven't—you missed some *lovely* pussy. But don't start crying yet, it all depends on what Nectar advises me to do. Who knows, by the time you have read this I may have fucked you!

***

Sugar's *exploits could fill a book so I've only given you a sneak preview, but this is not the last you will hear of the insatiable Brown sisters:* **Honey Comb, Nectar & Sugar.**

*****

Lightning Source UK Ltd.
Milton Keynes UK
UKOW031017180213

206439UK00007B/352/P